Yuit

Yuit

by Yvette Edmonds

Napoleon Publishing

Book design: Pamela Kinney

Cover design: Pamela Kinney

Cover illustration: Greg Ruhl

Project editor: Julian Woodford

Published by Napoleon Publishing Inc.
Toronto, Ontario, Canada

Printed in Canada

Canadian Cataloguing in Publication Data

Edmonds, Yvette, date
      Yuit

ISBN 0-929141-20-2

I. Inuit - Canada - Juvenile fiction. * II. Title

PS8559.D58Y85 1993   jC813'.54   C93-094438-0
PZ7.E46Yu   1993

Contents

For my father,
who believed,
and for his grandchildren,
Ilona and Geoffrey

Seals

This morning, when I looked out at the waters of the Murchison River from Grandpa's tent pitched on the river bank, I knew that the summer fishing season was over. It was early September, the time when the caribou were leaving the Arctic Circle to spend the winter in the south, near the tree-line, where they would find food.

Like the caribou, we too migrated with the seasons to hunt for food. Our whole tribe of over fifty Inuit was camped along this river near Shepherd Bay in the Northwest Territories. Our families had migrated here in the spring, leaving the melting sea ice on the shores of Shepherd Bay to catch and eat fish during the summer months. Soon, when the heavy snows fell and the caribou hunting season was over, our families would take down their tents and we would start our migration by dog sled and on foot, back to the sea ice where we would build our igloos and hunt seals.

As I looked up and down the river in the grey dawn, I could make out the shapes of the many tents the various families had pitched. I lived in a tent with Grandpa and Grandma. My father, who was Grandpa's son, had several children. Seeing that Grandpa and Grandma lived all alone, he had allowed them to adopt me. I would be company for them and, when I grew up and got married, my husband and I would look after them in their old age.

My best friend, Apitok, was also adopted by her grandparents and lived with them in their tent. Not all of us were adopted. Many of my other girlfriends lived with their parents. My older sisters and brothers still lived with my father and mother in their big tent further down the river. I visited my mother and father often, but even though I loved them, I felt closer to Grandpa and Grandma because they had raised me.

My father, older brothers and uncles, together with all the other hunters in the camp, were anxious to hunt the caribou before they disappeared. Early this morning, while it was still dark, they had hurried away with their rifles and dog sleds. When they returned, they would bring back enough caribou meat and skins to feed and clothe all the men, women and children in the camp.

I knew the hunters didn't take Grandpa with them because he was old and would slow them down. Only the strong, young hunters could go. The old men, the women and the children remained at home. We would wait eagerly for the hunters to return, hoping their sleds would be laden with meat for the women to cook, antler for the old men to carve and presents of caribou eyes for the children to suck on. We would keep a lookout and, as soon as one of us heard the sleds scraping ice in the distance as the hunters returned, we would alert the rest of the camp. Then we would all rush out of our tents, laughing and calling out with joy, as we ran to welcome the hunters back home and check on what they had caught.

Grandpa wanted to go hunting with the men and was sad at being left out. Of course, I knew they wouldn't take me, Liak, a girl, to hunt. I was to remain at home, along with Grandpa and Grandma and the rest of the villagers. But, like Grandpa, I felt restless.

"Grandpa," I said, trying to cheer him up, "why don't we go and set trap lines for white fox?"

His eyes immediately brightened. This was his favourite hobby when the weather got cold. "Yes," he said, "let's."

He told Grandma we would be leaving early

the next morning and that we would be gone several days. She smiled. She knew how much I enjoyed roaming the tundra with him.

We slipped away early the next morning and travelled north on the packed snow and ice for a couple of days. We walked, taking turns pulling our old dog sled, piled with our camping gear, after us. Sometimes, I sat on the sled and Grandpa pulled. When we arrived at the area where Grandpa knew white fox was plentiful, we set our traps in the snow. When we finished, we walked to the nearby lakes. Grandpa showed me how to cut ice holes in the frozen water and we fished for trout.

"Trout must be scarce this year," Grandpa muttered bleakly, after a few hours. "All morning, and we've only caught ten skinny ones!"

I knew why he was disappointed. He was ashamed to go back to our camp with such a small catch. He wanted to prove to our people he was still a good hunter.

I, too, didn't want to leave for home just yet. It was much more exciting hunting and camping with Grandpa. "Let's head for the sea ice on Shepherd Bay," I suggested, trying to keep him away from home longer.

He turned and looked out towards the waters of the bay. The sea water close to the shore had frozen, but the water further away hadn't. "It's a little too early, Liak."

"But we might get lucky and catch some seals!" I insisted.

He smiled at my insistence. "All right then," he said, "let's go!"

I was delighted. I helped him wrap the ten trout in seal skin. Then, with seal thongs, we lashed the bundle to our old sled and set off.

After walking half a day, surrounded by fields of snow and long, rolling hills of glistening white ice which reached down to the bay in the distance, we arrived at the edge of the sea ice where the land and water met. The ice cover on the water was thin and, where the water hadn't frozen yet, ice floes bobbed up and down or drifted slowly with the current.

"Grandpa, if we come across any seals, are you going to shoot them or will you harpoon them?"

"I'll harpoon them. I don't have too many bullets left. I'll save what I have for dangerous animals like polar bears, wolverines, and wolves. As soon as I trap some white fox, I'll go up to Spence Bay and trade their skins for more bullets. But you know, Liak," he said, scanning the expanse of sea ice before us, "I doubt we'll catch any seals today. They're all hiding under the ice cover."

But as he said it, we heard those unmistakable sounds. "Come," he gestured, and I caught the urgency in his voice.

"Seals are barking!" I whispered, feeling the excitement rise within me.

Swiftly, we moved in the direction of the barking. There, at the edge of the sea ice, we saw the dark, shadowy shapes of the seals. I was wondering if they were the huge, bearded seals when Grandpa's voice cut into my thoughts. "They're ringed seals," he said. He had sharp eyes.

The seals had climbed up onto the ice to sleep. They had a habit of waking up once or twice every minute to look out for danger.

As we looked, two of the mounds disappeared. But the largest one still remained. "We'll take that one."

I followed Grandpa's finger pointing to the largest mound.

"Hurry!" he whispered.

Since Grandpa was going to use his harpoon and not his gun, we had to creep up close enough to the remaining seal and then strike. We didn't want to alert it to our approach.

I did exactly what Grandpa did. I dropped to my tummy behind him and we both crawled carefully towards the seal. Every time it looked up, Grandpa and I, too, would look up and bark the deep, throaty bark of the seal. We would raise our right legs and move them as if they were hind flippers. We would scratch the ice with our snow knives, making the sounds of flippers scraping ice. When we were close enough, we waited until the seal closed its eyes. Then Grandpa jumped up and, running faster than the seal could slide into the water, he thrust his harpoon into it, killing it.

Yuit

Moments later, as we were about to bring our sled over to the dead seal, we heard scratching noises. It sounded as if something were trying to get away. We heard a little bark: "Aough!"

We both turned and saw a seal pup hidden in a bank of snow a few feet away.

I caught sight of the pup's eyes. At the same time, I saw Grandpa raise his hand and aim his harpoon at the pup. The pup was still looking at me, not even trying to move away. Its white fur gleamed like snowflakes; but it wasn't the colour of the fur that held me spellbound. It was the colour of the pup's eyes. They were pink, as if the baby seal had been crying. The pup needed me! Quickly, I flung myself upon it and shoved it away just as the tip of Grandpa's harpoon landed with a mighty thud on the ice beside us. I winced as some of the flying ice chips stung my cheeks.

"Liak!" Grandpa growled. "What do you think you're doing?"

I had never seen his wrinkled face come alive with so much anger.

"Don't you know any better?"

I shrank from his wrath and clung tightly to the pup. The warmth from its body gave me confidence. I would never let Grandpa kill it! Because of its eyes, pleading like a child's, the pup had become a person to me. "*Yuit, yuit,*" was all I could say as I fought back tears. I had to be brave. It wouldn't do to cry like a baby in front of Grandpa. "We Inuit never cry," he'd scold me. "Don't you know that we, the People of the Seal, are tough!" I'd show him! I was ten years old, with a mind of my own! "I'm naming my seal pup Yuit," I said, clinging even more tightly to the pup.

"*Yuit?*" He knitted his sparse, white eyebrows at me, a puzzled look creeping into his eyes. "Why do you want to give it a name like *Yuit*? *Yuit* means people!"

"I'm calling it Yuit because my seal pup is a person!"

"Come, come, Liak. Seals are food. They're not people!" He started to look amused.

It would be easier to reason with him now. "This seal pup isn't food, Grandpa. It's not like the other seals. It's a person! I don't know why, but I feel very strange about this pup. I can't explain it. All I know is it's a *yuit* and we mustn't eat it!"

"Liak, Liak," he shook his head, disbelievingly. "I should have left you at home with the women and the other girls to look after the babies."

"Grandpa, you know I don't like staying home cooped up in a tent! I prefer to come hunting with you." So that he wouldn't send me back home, I tried to make myself useful. I pointed to the seal cow. "What shall we do about the seal?"

He turned and looked at the dead seal lying a few feet away. There was blood on the ice around it. "We'll have to drag it home. Aren't Grandma's eyes going to sparkle when she sees so much food!" Then he looked up at the dark clouds rolling in, throwing shadows upon us. "We'll have to hurry, Liak. Come and help me."

I made sure Yuit was safe in a hollow in the ice, surrounded by piles of snow. "Stay here," I said, as I patted it. "As soon as I'm finished, I'll come and play with you."

With his knife, Grandpa made a slit in the cow's belly. I also helped cut through the blubber with my knife.

Grandpa pulled out the liver. "Here." He cut a big chunk and handed it to me.

Together, we ate the raw liver hungrily. We hadn't eaten since last night. We cupped our hands and drank some of the seal blood. It was still warm and delicious. When we finished, I helped Grandpa pin the seal's skin together with a sharp bone pin.

"This is a big cow," he said. "There's enough blubber on her to keep my grandchildren happy!"

I thought of the times I visited my cousins in the igloos and tents of my aunts and uncles when the hunting season was bad and meat and fish were scarce. We, the older children, used to suck on lumps of ice to keep from feeling hungry, but my smaller cousins would refuse to do so and would cry with hunger until they fell asleep.

"Yes," I nodded. "It'll keep their bellies full. Otherwise, they cry and I can't sleep at night."

Grandpa smiled affectionately. "Ah, Liak, Liak," he said. "I wouldn't know what to do without you to keep me company. Life can be lonely for an old man." Then he sighed. "Soon, my body will lie upon the ice with stones around it."

"Hush, Grandpa! Don't talk like that! I know you're stronger and braver than some of the younger hunters in our camp!"

"You're good for me, Liak," he said fondly. Then his face grew serious. "But no one else thinks that way. I couldn't go hunting caribou with your uncles and father this morning because they don't think I'm a good hunter anymore." A sad look crept into his eyes. "My body is no longer as fast and strong as it used to be."

"But look at what you've just killed!" I pointed to the cow. "A seal!"

"That's true." He looked brighter. "I never thought we'd be lucky enough to catch a seal today."

We strapped the seal cow to the sled with seal thong, and pulled it to where the pup lay.

"There's something strange about this pup," he said. "Pups bite, but this one didn't bite at all."

"That's because it's a person! People don't bite!"

"You're a funny one," he chuckled.

Then I saw him stiffen. He stared at the pup, and he froze with fear.

The Sea Goddess Nuliajuk

"Grandpa! What's the matter?"

"Those eyes!" he said hoarsely. "Those eyes!"

"What about those eyes? What are you talking about?"

"The pup's eyes are pink!"

"I know! That's because Yuit's been crying. It didn't want to be harpooned!"

"Liak," he said severely, "this pup hasn't been crying. It's an albino! Only albinos have pink eyes like that!"

"So? What's wrong with an albino?"

"Albinos bring bad luck."

"What do you mean, Grandpa? Surely Yuit won't harm us!"

"Liak, many, many years ago, before you were born, some hunters harpooned a white whale in the Arctic Ocean. Its eyes were large and pink. The hunters knew it was an albino, and that it would bring bad luck. They should have let it go, but they were so hungry, they killed it. On the shore, they skinned it, cut up the meat and blubber, and took it all home to their families to eat. Soon after that, the hunters caught the white man's disease and died."

"But Yuit's a seal, not a whale!"

"It doesn't matter. An albino is an albino, whether it's a seal or a whale. You must let Yuit go."

I kicked at the snow with my caribou boots. The silence hung heavy, like a thick fog, between Grandpa and me. I didn't want anything as terrible as the white man's disease to kill our people. I loved them too much. Yet, I loved Yuit too and I didn't want to give it up. My heart was being pulled two ways, and I wanted to go both ways. A thought flashed through my head. "I'm glad Yuit's an albino," I said suddenly.

"Why?"

"Because no Inuit will dare to eat it, and it'll be safe."

"That's right. So you can stop worrying now and let it go."

"No! Please don't make me do that!"

"If you don't, the Sea Goddess, Nuliajuk, will become angry. She lives at the bottom of the ocean and controls all the sea creatures. Albinos belong to her. If you displease her by taking Yuit away from her, she'll drive away all the seals and fish, and our people will starve."

I had heard about the cruel ways of Nuliajuk from all the hunters in our camp. When the men went away on long trips in their *kayaks* and larger *umiaks* to the Arctic Ocean to hunt seals and whales, Nuliajuk would whip up sudden storms, making the waves so big, they could overturn the boats and drown all the hunters. Other times, she would hide the sea animals deep within the folds of her watery robes so that the hunters wouldn't be able to find them. They would be forced to go home empty-handed. A hunter was supposed to provide food for his family. If he couldn't, he would hang his head in shame. Sometimes, he would feel so useless, he would commit suicide.

"We must appease Nuliajuk," Grandpa reminded me.

"I know," I said, feeling sad. I looked out at the miles upon miles of sea ice covering the ocean. If only I knew where Nuliajuk lived, I'd go and talk to her. If she loved the sea animals, surely she'd understand my love for Yuit. "Nuliajuk," I whispered, "I want to keep Yuit as my pet. I want to be kind to it and look after it. Please tell me what to do. I don't want to make you angry."

A Premonition

Just then, as I was still staring out at the expanse of white sea ice before me, Yuit looked up at me and barked, "Aough! Aough!" "I think it's telling us it doesn't want to be sent away." I bent down and stroked it. Then I perked up. "Grandpa, the pup's a female!"

"Why, so she is!"

"It's like having a baby sister! Now I won't feel so lonely."

"Aough! Aough!"

"See, she agrees!"

But Grandpa didn't agree. "There are enough babies in our camp for you to play with, Liak."

"But it's not the same as having a pet!"

"Come along, now, Liak." Grandpa was getting impatient. "We must be on our way. Let Yuit go. The Sea Goddess will look after her."

I knew I had to obey. "Run along, Yuit," I said, tapping her flippers and pushing her towards the open water. "Go and see Nuliajuk. She's

16

waiting for you."

"Aough! Aough!" She refused to budge.

It suddenly dawned on me that the pup was talking to me. How I wished I could understand the language of seals! Was Nuliajuk answering my prayer through the pup, telling me that Yuit could stay with me as my pet? I began to feel strangely happy. Yet, I didn't dare hope for too much. I'd better do as Grandpa said, or he'd get angry.

"Shoo, Yuit, shoo! Go home to the Sea Goddess. Scat! Run along!"

"Aough! Aough!" She refused again. She looked at the dead seal.

"Grandpa, she doesn't want to leave. Is that her mother we've killed?"

"Yes."

As we watched, Yuit pulled herself across the ice to the sled, using her flippers and strong belly muscles.

"I'm sorry we took your mother away from you, Yuit," I said, feeling a twinge of pity for the small seal. "Grandpa, would Yuit starve now that we've killed her mother?"

"No, she looks like she's fully weaned, and more than four months old. She should be able to live on her own now. Otherwise, I would be really afraid. She'd die of starvation. It would be our fault. The Sea Goddess would punish us."

"Not even if we promised to feed Yuit so she'd stay alive?"

"No," he shook his head. "It's impossible to force-feed a seal pup that hasn't been weaned.

"Poor thing. She's just as helpless as my baby cousins!"

"Aough! Aough!" Yuit nudged the sled with her snout.

"I think she wants to sit on it. I've given her her freedom, but she doesn't want it. Look! She's nodding!"

"That's a strange pup," Grandpa scratched his head. He knelt down and patted the sides of the pup's stomach. "You're a fat one, aren't you?"

My hopes rose. He was talking to the pup as if she were a child, patting her the same way he patted the babies at home. "She's pretty, isn't she?" I, too, knelt down beside him.

"Yes," he nodded. He watched me pull my fingers through the pup's fur. "I think you like her because of her white fur, don't you? And her pink nose. She's different. If she were mottled and ordinary-looking, like the usual ringed seal pups, you wouldn't care about her."

"It's not just the white fur that makes me want to keep her, Grandpa. It's something else. I don't know what it is. I wish I could explain it." I felt confused. I was struggling with so many ideas I couldn't put into words.

"Grandpa, inside me, I have this feeling that Yuit is going to do something special for me..." I saw him looking at me as if I were out of my mind. I stopped trying to explain myself.

"You think too much," he scolded. "Stop thinking and behave more like the other little girls in our camp."

I was afraid to share any more of my thoughts with him. He'd only ridicule me. How I wished someone would help me find the answers to all these questions in my head! Would my life change because of Yuit? If so, how? Was the Sea Goddess coming back in the form of the white seal pup to test my kindness? Was it my mission to save Yuit?

The more I thought about it, the more I began to feel there was a connection between Nuliajuk, Yuit, and me. "Grandpa, please tell me the legend of the Sea Goddess once again," I asked.

"All right," he said, his voice livening up. He enjoyed telling legends and I was a good listener. He sat down comfortably on the ice beside the sled with me and Yuit. He took a deep breath.

"Once upon a time," he began, "some Inuit wanted to leave their village and move to better hunting grounds in search of food. In order to do so, they had first to cross the waters of

Sherman Inlet. They tied their *kayaks* together and made rafts. They were in a hurry to leave.

A little girl called Nuliajuk also lived in the village. Because she was an orphan, no one cared about her. She had no relatives to help or protect her. Like all the other little boys and girls, she, too, jumped onto one of the rafts. But since the raft was small, and since there wasn't enough room for everyone, the villagers grabbed her and threw her into the water. She swam frantically back to the raft and clung to its edge. When she tried to climb back in, some of the villagers took their knives and cut off her fingers. She sank to the bottom of the inlet. As she did so, a miracle occurred. Her fingers bobbed up around the raft and became seals. That was how the first seals came to be.

"Aough! Aough!" Yuit barked, as if agreeing.

"At the bottom of the inlet, she turned into a Sea Goddess. Because seals were formed from her fingers, she became the mother of all sea creatures. She also became the mistress of all land animals. The bottom of the ocean became her home. From there, she rules over all the tundra's animals and controls us through them."

"Poor Nuliajuk," I sighed, when he had finished. "Our people shouldn't have rejected her. Is that why she plays such cruel tricks on us?"

"Yes. She has very little love for the Inuit because we treated her so badly."

"She can be kind, too, can't she? She provides us with game!"

"True, but first we have to soothe her; which is why our shamans have to dive down so often to her sea home to plead with her and beg forgiveness."

The more I thought about the legend, the more I became convinced it was my duty to save Yuit. In doing so, I would be helping to make up for the past cruelty of the Inuit towards the little orphan girl. In return, Nuliajuk was going to help me do something that would be important for me. Even though I didn't know yet what it was, I felt the excitement flow through me.

I Feel Lonely

"Grandpa," I tried again, "I've given Yuit her freedom, even pushed her to the water, but she doesn't want to go." I saw him narrow his eyes. It made me feel nervous. "Can Yuit stay with me as my pet, please?" I rushed my words.

"No." He shook his head.

"But…" I couldn't finish my sentence. I felt as if my heart had been harpooned.

"The *Angatkok* will never give you permission to keep an albino seal pup." His voice was firm. "Our shaman is very careful never to anger Nuliajuk."

I wiped away a tear.

Something made me look up at Grandpa then. His face was lined and sad. Poor Grandpa, I realized suddenly. It hurts him to refuse me.

A wind rose, blowing the thin strands of grey hair about Grandpa's face. It made me aware of how old he really was, and of how fond I was of him. As an Inuit, I accepted death. It happened to everyone. Death was part of living. Yet, if Grandpa left this snowy world of the tundra, there would be an empty place in my heart. Hurriedly, I brushed the thought of death away, but the knowledge that I would one day lose Grandpa made me feel lonely. If only he would let me keep Yuit, I would have something to fill the void his death would leave.

I wondered if Nuliajuk had ever felt as lonely and confused as I was now feeling. Thinking about the little orphan girl made me feel very close to Yuit. Yuit was also an orphan. Now I knew why I wanted to keep the pup. Giving her love, touching her, patting her, running my fingers through her silky, shimmering fur, made me feel less lonely. Yuit was the pet I'd been searching for all my life. How could I explain all of this to Grandpa without him thinking me foolish?

Usually, it didn't bother me that I was adopted. Now, because Nuliajuk was on my mind, I began to fret about it. I didn't mind being adopted, but I often wished Grandpa and Grandma had adopted another little girl as well to keep me company.

When I was younger, I used to visit my parents' igloo every day to play with my two older sisters. I hardly knew my brothers, because they were always away hunting with my father. It was my sisters that I clung to. We would play our favourite game called "mother". We would go around the camp looking for stray puppies. These we would carry in the back pouches of our caribou jackets as if they were babies. We would hop slowly from one foot to the other, the way mothers do, and sing Netsilik songs. Soon, the puppies would be lulled to sleep just like babies. But because dogs ate so much blubber and fish and were expensive to keep, there weren't too many puppies in the camp.

With no puppies to cradle, my sisters and I used to wander in the tundra, especially during the summer months, looking for other pets to play with. We would chase lemmings and ermine, capturing them as they ran under the rocks for cover. But lemmings and ermine didn't make good pets because they refused to go to sleep quietly in our pouches like the puppies did. They would scramble wildly all over us, squeaking with fear. We gave up trying to train them as pets. They were too small and restless, running away from us all the time.

Now that my sisters were older, they no longer played with me. They stayed at home with my mother all day, learning how to cook, how to do housework, how to mind babies and how to sew winter clothing from caribou skins. All this was in preparation for the time when they would get married, which I knew would be soon. With no sisters to play with, I felt left out.

Perhaps going to school would be the answer. I had heard about school from my distant cousins in Spence Bay. When I visited them there, on one of Grandpa's trading trips, they pulled me aside excitedly. "We're learning so many interesting things in school," they told me. "Things like drawing animals, learning to read, write, sing, and play games. We've also made lots of friends our own age!"

Once, when I had told Grandpa I envied them because they were lucky enough to go to the government school there, and that I, too, wanted to go to school, he became angry. He was old-fashioned and believed in Inuit tradition. "Why do you want to change and be different from the other girls in our tribe?" he had chided. "There's no need for you to go to school. Every Inuit girl should stay at home and learn to be a good wife. Those cousins of yours have been putting silly ideas into your head!"

After that, I didn't dare to mention school to him again. It was hopeless. There was no school here in Shepherd Bay. I would have to leave home and go to Spence Bay and that was out of the question. It was too far away, and my life was here with my people. So I put all thought of school out of my mind.

Right now, I knew what I needed most was a pet to teach tricks, a pet I could romp with. How wonderful that would be! Without Yuit, I would feel as trapped as that black fly I saw this morning, frozen in a lump of river ice.

Just For A Day?

I was still standing on the sea ice, thoughts flying in and out of my head like snowflakes in a storm, looking at Yuit and worrying about her, when Grandpa cut into my thoughts.

"Come along, Liak," he was saying. "You brood too much. What are you thinking about now?"

"It's about Yuit. We've done everything to chase her away, but she refuses to go. I think she's lonely now that we've killed her mother. Can I look after her, please, just for one day?" There was pleading in my voice.

As Grandpa gazed at me, the annoyance left his eyes, and they became filled once again with their usual warmth. "Ah, Liak, Liak," he said. "You're a scheming, little one! Yes, you may keep Yuit for one day. But remember," he shook his finger at me, "only for *one* day. Then we must force her to go back to Nuliajuk before the Sea Goddess finds out her albino is with us. I don't want to risk any punishment. Do you understand?"

"Yes, Grandpa! Thank you!" My heart leapt. I turned to the pup. "You can stay with me for one whole day, Yuit!" I threw my arms around her.

Grandpa held his head up into the rising wind. "It looks like we're in for another harsh winter," he said. "I saw the geese fly south a couple of days ago. They were leaving early."

"I saw them leave too. They made a big, grey 'V' in the sky, and I could hear them honking as they flapped their wings. Brrrrrrrr," I shivered. I tied my hood tighter about my head.

The wind, blowing in from the cold arctic wastes of the northwest, was picking up speed, bringing snow with it. Winter was starting to get a firm grip on the tundra, painting everything white. I was glad I had worn my two suits of caribou skin. The outer skin had thick, coarse fur, but the inner one felt nice and warm with its soft fur next to my own skin.

"Hurry," Grandpa said. "We must leave for home while there's still light."

"Too bad we couldn't bring the dogs to pull the sled. It'll be heavy to pull with the seal cow on it."

"It was more important that the dogs went with your father and brothers to pull the caribou meat and skins home."

I knew that because dogs were expensive to feed, two families shared three dogs between them. "One day," I said, hope rising within me, "every Inuit family will be able to afford its own dog team. And then, you and Father won't have to share your dogs."

"That will only happen when we are no longer poor," Grandpa replied. There was no hope in his voice. "We have always been poor."

I knew he wasn't complaining. For generations, our family had fished and hunted in Shepherd Bay. This was our home, cold and harsh, but still our home. Grandpa never grumbled about his struggle for survival under harsh conditions. He knew that such conditions made the Inuit hardy and brave, and he was proud of these qualities.

"Aough! Aough!" Yuit barked. I turned. The falling snow had covered her fur, barely showing her eyes.

"Aough! Aough!" I laughed, imitating her. I brushed the snow off her. "Yes, Yuit, we'll be leaving soon, and you'll be coming with us!"

I saw Grandpa staring at the dead seal, deep in thought. "You know, Liak," he said, "because I have so few bullets left, I don't think it'll be wise to drag the cow home."

"Why?" I was reluctant to leave all that food

behind.

"Because the smell of seal meat and blood on the sled might attract polar bears. We wouldn't be safe if one of them attacked us. Let's cache the cow."

First, I helped Grandpa cut enough seal steaks for our journey home. We wrapped these in seal skin and tied the bundle to the sled, together with the trout we had caught earlier this morning.

Next, I helped him find a safe spot on the ice for the cache. We dug a deep hole and placed the cow in it. We filled the hole with blocks of ice and cemented the blocks together with snow. We shoveled the old snow back on top of these blocks until we had covered the hole.

"Now, no wild animals will pillage our precious meat!" Grandpa stood back to admire our work.

The surface snow didn't even look disturbed.

There was no need to mark the site because Grandpa knew his hunting grounds well. When he returned with the dog team many days from now, he would be able to find the cache, even with his eyes closed.

The Igloo

After caching the cow, we walked over to the sled and made a comfortable bed of seal skins on it for Yuit. We lifted Yuit and placed her in it. We wrapped more seal skin around her and tied her securely to the sled so she wouldn't fall off, no matter how fast we pulled it.

"Ready?" Grandpa turned to me.

"Yes," I nodded. "Yuit," I called to her over my shoulder, "we're going to take you for a nice, long ride!"

"Aough! Aough!" she barked excitedly.

Grandpa and I laughed. We picked up the thick, seal skin thong usually strapped to the front of the old dog sled and hauled it away, running through the fresh-falling snow.

Every once in a while, I'd glance back. "We'll be home soon, Yuit!"

We were hurrying south from Shepherd Bay to Inglis Bay. Then, we would turn east and travel inland to our family camp on the banks of the Murchison River.

We ran for several hours, panting in the cold. It was getting colder and windier by the minute. Heads bowed, we braced ourselves against the wind. The snowflakes got larger and heavier. The strong, icy wind swirled masses of these snowflakes wildly around, sweeping the snow on the ground into long drifts. The drifts got thicker and higher, making it difficult for us to pull our sled over them.

I glanced back anxiously at Yuit. She was bobbing up and down uncomfortably with the bumpy movement of the sled.

Soon, the snow became so thick, we couldn't even see an arm's length in front of us.

"I didn't think there was going to be a snowstorm today," Grandpa said, snow swirling round his mouth as he spoke. "The sky looked so clear this morning." He squinted through the cloud of snowflakes at me. "Are you sure you're all right?"

"I'm fine. I just hope Yuit's all right." I cast another backward glance at her.

"Don't worry about Yuit. Seals can take worse weather than this."

We struggled doggedly on. But because the wind was so strong and the snow so heavy, we didn't get very far.

"I'm afraid we won't make it even halfway home today," Grandpa said. "It's dangerous to travel when you can't see where you're going. For one thing, we could be going around in circles, and for another, we could be attacked by wolves or hungry polar bears. They'd kill us before we even spotted them. We'll have to stop and camp."

We found a spot where the snow was hard-packed. It would give us all the snow blocks we needed. With our snow knives, we hacked out several blocks.

As I handed Grandpa the blocks, he stacked them up around him in a continuous, circular row that wound upwards in smaller and smaller circles to form our dome-shaped igloo. He left a small hole in the ceiling for stale air to escape.

"And now, if you'll help me build our sleeping platform," he said, "we'll be finished."

I shoveled loose snow and packed it hard against the inside wall of the igloo, opposite the low entrance. I climbed onto this low mound and packed it down even further by jumping up and down on it several times until I had formed a flat-topped platform.

"I'll get our sleeping skins now, Grandpa," I offered.

I crawled out of the opening and ran to the sled. I unpacked the caribou skins. I raced back into the igloo and laid them on top of the sleeping platform. "There! Now we'll be safe from the snowstorm!"

"You're a good helper," Grandpa nodded, looking approvingly at my efforts.

I beamed. I loved nothing better than helping him.

Left to Die

While Grandpa unpacked his camping gear and carried everything inside the igloo, I brought Yuit in and romped with her on the ice floor.

Grandpa stuck his harpoon in the outer wall of the igloo. He placed the fish and the seal steaks in a shallow cache just inside the entrance. There we could get at the food easily whenever we were hungry. He closed the entrance with a block of ice. "No wild animals will bother us now," he muttered, as he came in.

Yuit watched him, curious, as he lit the storm lantern. "Aough! Aough!" she barked.

"Now we can see what we're doing, can't we!" I laughed.

I got up to cook our dinner. I could see Grandpa was hungry. So was I, after all the running I'd done.

I lit the little kerosene stove. I half-filled the small iron pot with pieces of ice I had scraped from the floor, and placed the pot on the stove. I threw in some seal steaks and frozen seal blood. As the ice in the pot melted and began to bubble, the delicious smell of cooking seal meat filled the igloo.

Grandpa came and sat near me. Together, we watched our dinner boil.

"It'll be ready soon," I said, as I turned to him. My heart sank when I saw his face. There was a deep frown on it. He wasn't looking at me, but vaguely at the bubbling soup, which he didn't seem to see. Something was bothering him. "What's the matter, Grandpa?"

He continued to stare at the bubbles. A deep sigh escaped his lips, like some dark waters rushing out of a gorge. "There's something I have to tell you, Liak," he said at last, still without looking at me. "Something I've kept secret for a long time."

"Is it about me?"

"Yes."

"Is it bad?"

He didn't meet my eyes.

"Tell me!"

"Liak," he sighed again, as if what he was about to tell me was going to be painful for both of us, "while you were still in your mother's womb, your father said I could adopt you. Your parents had several children and their igloo was crammed. I had lots of room because Grandma and I lived alone. I told him I would only adopt you if you were a boy. I wanted to train a boy as a hunter. My sons were grown. I was lonely. An adopted son would be company for me in my old age. When you were born, and I found out you were a girl, I was bitterly disappointed. So disappointed that I refused to adopt you. Your father already had too many girls. He didn't want another. He wasn't hunting enough food to feed so many mouths. Boys were more useful than girls. They remained with you and helped you hunt. Girls were different. Just when they reached the age when they could be useful around the igloo, they got married and left you. Since I refused to adopt you and since your father couldn't afford to keep you, he ordered your mother to kill you. She placed you naked outside their igloo at night so that you would freeze to death. I heard your cries. My heart, which had remained like a solid block of ice all along, suddenly began to melt. I went outside and picked you up. You were blue with cold and very close to death. I brought you inside my igloo and bundled you up in a piece of soft caribou calf skin. With the warmth, you soon recovered. You grew into a strong baby. Instead of leaving you entirely in the care of Grandma and letting her raise you like a little girl, I took charge of you. I raised you as if you were a boy, teaching you how to hunt, and taking you on long trips with me. I haven't been fair to you, Liak. After all, you're a girl, and I should let Grandma take over now. I mustn't be selfish. Grandma will train you to cook, sew, keep house and look after babies, duties which every Inuit girl should know."

I was so choked, I couldn't say anything. To cover up my misery, I pretended to stir the boiling seal meat.

I sensed Yuit's pink eyes on me. They were giving me strength. I calmed down enough to speak. "I like the way you've been raising me, Grandpa, and I want to continue learning to hunt. Something tells me I have to. Please don't make me stay at home!"

"But you have to learn to do housework, child."

"I already know how to do housework! See." I pointed to the bubbling seal meat. "I'm cooking your dinner!"

"But you must learn to sew caribou skins. Every Inuit girl must have that skill."

"That's not difficult! I've watched Grandma sew, and it won't take me long to learn!" Then a thought came to me. "If I sew you a caribou hunting jacket, will you continue to take me hunting with you?"

"Liak, please, you must listen to me."

Yes, I was listening, but my mind was preoccupied with the way I was feeling. My blood was chilled. And it was chilled like the blood is chilled when a wolf calls and you know it is hungry. But this was worse than that. I had to find out the truth, even if it hurt me. "Grandpa, are you glad you adopted me?"

Safe for Tonight

For what seemed like the longest moment I'd ever known, Grandpa stared at the yellow flames dancing beneath the soup pot. Then he turned to me, and there was a gentle smile in his black eyes. "Yes, Liak," he nodded, "I'm glad I adopted you." His voice was full of love.

Immediately, I felt reassured and happy. My appetite returned, and so did his.

I busied myself filling two tin mugs with seal-meat soup. "Here, Grandpa." I handed him his. He took it and ate. It felt good to see him eat the food I'd cooked with so much relish.

"Aough! Aough!" Yuit barked, telling me it was time to feed her too.

I gave her one of the frozen lake trout from the cache. As I watched, she gobbled the fish down whole. I couldn't help giggling. She must have been really starving!

"I'm going to brew you some tea now," I said, turning to Grandpa.

"Tea? Did you say tea?" His eyes lit up. He didn't think we had any left. Tea was his favourite drink.

"Of course!" I showed him the handful of tea leaves I'd carried in my pocket. "Grandma saved this for you. She told me it was the last little bit left. It should last several brewings, if I'm careful."

"As soon as I trap some white fox, I'll go up to Spence Bay and trade their skins for more tea," he promised.

I filled the black, sooty kettle with snow and put it on the primus stove. When the snow melted and the water started to boil, I added the tea leaves. I rinsed out the two dirty, tin mugs with snow and filled them with hot tea.

Grandpa took his mug and went and sat on the sleeping platform. He liked to make himself comfortable whenever he drank his tea.

I took mine and joined Yuit on the floor. "Yuit, tomorrow morning, as soon as I get up, I'm going to teach you tricks!"

"Tricks? What tricks?" Grandpa was surprised. "I didn't know you knew how to teach seals tricks!"

"Tricks that the missionary told me about. That missionary whose life you saved, when he was mauled by a polar bear."

"Father Dubois of Spence Bay?"

"Yes. He told me about those tricks while he was recovering in our igloo and you were away hunting."

"He was lucky I arrived just in time to chase that old bear away!" Grandpa chuckled, remembering. "Otherwise, he would have been killed for sure."

He started to yawn. It was time to go to bed.

I took the empty mug away from him. I removed all the tea leaves from the kettle, squeezed them, and put them on a piece of seal skin to dry overnight. I would brew the same leaves again tomorrow.

I went to the pup and patted her. "Good night, Yuit. You'll be comfortable here on the floor."

Grandpa turned off the storm lantern, and we all settled down for the night. Grandpa fell asleep as soon as he put his head down on his folded jacket. I could hear him snoring. But I couldn't sleep. I kept tossing and turning, worrying about Yuit's fate tomorrow. Grandpa had said I could only keep her for one day, and tomorrow, that one day would be up. I couldn't bear the thought of letting her go.

Outside, I could hear the wind bashing the snow furiously against our igloo walls and, in the distance, I could hear wolves howling, as they prowled around looking for food. I looked at the faint outline of Yuit lying quietly on the ice floor and was glad that for tonight at least, she was safe with me in my igloo.

Tricks

The next morning, Yuit came over to where I lay on the sleeping platform. "Aough! Aough!" she raised herself and poked at my face with her snout.

I opened my eyes; I tried to rub the sleep out of them with my fists. I yawned. I was still tired after a sleepless night and the nightmares I had had about wolves attacking and eating Yuit. Slowly, I crawled out from under my skins and plunked myself down on the floor beside her. I lay there until I was fully awake. Then I got up and lit the stove to make tea.

Grandpa was already shoveling snow out of the entrance so we could get out. "It's still snowing," he grumbled.

I glanced out, and was secretly pleased. I wished it would never stop snowing. It meant we could stay here longer in the igloo with Yuit.

We sat down on the ice floor for breakfast. Grandpa and I drank the tea which I had saved and chewed on frozen fillets of raw fish, while Yuit gobbled her trout down whole.

After breakfast, Grandpa continued to stare bleakly out through the entrance. It was still snowing.

"Would you like your carving things?" I asked, thinking to distract him, hoping that somehow this would prolong our stay.

"Yes," he nodded, looking less bleak. He enjoyed carving toy guns, knives and animals out of antler. These he would barter for raisins and chocolates when he went to Spence Bay on his trading trips. Both of us loved sweet things.

While he carved, I turned to the pup. "Time for your first lesson now, Yuit! Do as I do!"

I lay on the floor in the middle of the igloo and rolled from my tummy to my back, over and over. Yuit merely watched and barked without doing anything. "Here, I'll show you." I held her with both hands and rolled her over and over on the ice all around the igloo.

"Aough! Aough!" she complained, not sure she liked being pushed around like that.

"Come along, Yuit. You can do it."

Soon, after many tries, and much to my delight, she began to get the hang of it and rolled over and over on her own.

"Look at her, Grandpa!"

He glanced at her, but there was no pleasure

in his eyes. He was more interested in staring out of the igloo to see when it would stop snowing.

I was disappointed. I wanted him to be impressed with Yuit so he'd allow me to keep her. I'd try harder. "Now Yuit, do this." I clapped my hands.

"Aough! Aough!" she barked and started to roll over.

"No. No. This." I started clapping again.

She watched me with a confused look in her pink eyes.

I suddenly realized she was unable to clap because she was lying on her tummy, and the ice floor was in the way of her front flippers. I lifted her up on her hind flippers. "Now clap." I showed her how again. To my surprise, she actually began to clap. The sound of her flippers went "flap, flap, flap, flap" around the igloo.

Grandpa looked up at the noise, and some of the grimness disappeared from his eyes. "You shouldn't confuse the poor pup by teaching her things only humans can do," he said.

"Oh, but Grandpa, look at how fast she learns! Go on, Yuit," I prodded, "show Grandpa how clever you are."

She began beating her flippers together again, "flap, flap, flap."

Grandpa smiled the way he did when a baby in the camp started to walk on its own for the first time.

Then he glanced out through the entrance, and that impatient look came back into his eyes.

Undaunted, I turned to Yuit. "I'm going to teach you another trick." I ducked out of the entrance and picked up a handful of snow. I moulded this into a snowball as I came back into the igloo.

"You mustn't get too attached to the pup," Grandpa warned.

I ignored what he said. "Watch me carefully," I told Yuit. "I want you to balance this snowball on your nose like this, see." I put the ball on my nose and tried to balance it, but it fell off.

"Aough! Aough!" Yuit sounded as if she were laughing at me.

"Well, see if *you* can do any better!" I placed the snowball on her nose. To my utter surprise, she balanced it. She even moved around the igloo without dropping it. "Good girl!" I was thrilled. I noticed Grandpa looking at us. "And now, Yuit, I want you to learn to sing with me."

"Aough! Aough!" She was eager to join in.

"That's right, Yuit. Sing Aough! Aough! along with me."

I began to chant a lullaby Grandma used to

sing to me when I was little. Yuit accompanied me, singing her Aough Aoughs in time to the beat.

"Wonderful!" I hugged her at the end of the song. "Grandpa, did you like our duet?"

When I turned to look at him, my mouth fell open. He was looking eagerly out of the entrance. There was a happy look on his face.

"Liak," he said, turning to me, "it's stopped snowing! It's time for you to return Yuit to the Sea Goddess."

With that, he got up and started making preparations to leave.

Camp!

Ifelt so miserable, I couldn't speak. Yet, if I wanted to keep Yuit, I'd better speak up now. If I didn't, I'd lose her forever. "Grandpa," I begged, "Yuit is special. She's not just like any other seal pup. Nuliajuk wants me to keep her as my pet. I know it! Please let her stay with me!"

"You see, already you've grown attached to her!" he cried out, crankily. "I knew I shouldn't have let you keep her, even for one day!" But when he saw my eyes brim over, his face softened. "I've a suggestion," he said instead. "We'll leave Yuit here in the igloo with some fish. When we return later with the dog team to fetch the cached seal, we'll check in on her. If she's still here, you can take her home. If she isn't, we'll know she has returned to Nuliajuk."

"But if we leave her behind, the wolves will kill her for sure! And when Nuliajuk finds out we didn't protect her albino, she'll punish us!"

A worried look appeared on his face.

"Aough! Aough!" Yuit, too, looked up at him, her pink eyes holding the same urgency I had in my voice.

All of a sudden, something seemed to be happening to Grandpa. He began to look strange. His eyes went blank. His body swayed from side-to-side as if he were experiencing a dizzy spell. His hands flew up to clasp his head. He looked as if he were wrestling with something in his mind, struggling to pull things out and think clearly. Then his knees buckled under him and he slowly fell to the ground in a faint.

"Grandpa!" I rushed to him and held him in my arms, frightened for him. "Sea Goddess, please let nothing happen to him!"

"Aough! Aough!" Yuit came over and continued to talk softly to him.

Slowly Grandpa opened his eyes. He blinked, trying to focus on Yuit and me. Then, he slowly sat up. "It's nothing." He brushed off his fainting spell. "I was just a little tired." He stared at Yuit, looking as if he were coming out of a deep sleep. Then he turned and looked at me. "Yes," he said, "you may keep Yuit."

"Thank you, Grandpa!"

"But," he cautioned, "you'll never get past the *Angatkok*."

"Not even if the shaman were to swim down to Nuliajuk's home and plead with her to let me keep Yuit?"

"No." He shook his head. "He'll never do that. Our *Angatkok* is very strict. If he forbids you to keep Yuit, there's nothing I can do. He has the power to banish you from our tribe, if you disobey him. He even has the power to order you to be put to death. And I don't want that to happen to you." His voice choked.

Panic shot through me. "I know," I said. I, too, was terrified of angering the *Angatkok*. But, for the moment, because my joy at being able to keep Yuit was so great, I was able to overcome my fear. "You can stay with me Yuit!" I hopped and skipped around her.

She followed me around the igloo as I helped Grandpa pack our camping things back on the sled. When we lifted her and strapped her to the sled, she protested, "Aough! Aough!"

"I don't think she wants to be pulled, Grandpa. I think she'll have more fun walking with us."

"If we had more time, she could. But it's going to snow again, and I want to get home before it does. She'll just have to get used to being pulled." He sounded grumpy.

He grabbed the thong and dragged the sled out through the low entrance of the igloo, while

I pushed from behind. I noticed that he was limping a little. I hadn't seen that limp before. What's the matter with your leg, Grandpa?"

"It's nothing," he said, brushing me aside, "just an old hunting injury acting up."

We trudged off through the snow, pulling the sled after us. Last night's thick blanket of snow made travelling difficult. We kept sinking knee-deep, and spent a lot of time digging ourselves out. Grandpa found this tiring, but I found it fun. I loved burrowing in the soft snow like a rabbit. I was in no hurry to get home. I wanted to stay away from the *Angatkok* for as long as I could.

"Liak, you're slowing us down," Grandpa complained.

I could see he wasn't really angry with me. Even though he kept saying he was in a hurry to get home, I noticed that he, too, was slowing down. He, too, was reluctant to face the *Angatkok*.

The closer we got to home, the more tense we became. I shivered. Not with the cold, but with nervousness. What would the *Angatkok* do to me?

Just before we rounded the last bend in the river, Grandpa suggested we stop and rest. It would give us a chance to steel ourselves before we finally came face to face with the shaman.

We untied Yuit and let her wander around. Both of us watched her in deep silence. Soon, even Yuit became depressed. She stopped moving around and watched us with quiet, pink eyes.

Then, all of a sudden, her eyes sparked up. "Aough! Aough!" she barked, as she came over to us and prodded us with her snout. She seemed to be telling us to get up and go. She herself led the way by climbing back onto the sled.

"I don't know what *she's* got to look forward to," Grandpa muttered testily.

Grudgingly, we both got up and tied her down securely on her bed of skins.

All joy about going home seeped out of me as we pulled the sled to the top of the bend. If only it would snow again, I thought despairingly, we could stay away for another night. I looked up at the sky; it was clear.

We were moving around the bend now.

And then the shout went up. "Here come Liak and Grandpa!"

Discovered!

A group of children were running towards us. More were pouring out of their *karmaqs*, calling out excitedly: "Liak and Grandpa are here! Liak and Grandpa are here!"

In the short time we had been away, the tents had become too cold to live in, and had given way to *karmaqs* with their tent roofs and walls cut from slabs of river ice. Since we villagers always helped each other, some of them had helped put the ice walls up for Grandma while Grandpa and I were away.

With relief, I noticed that only the children, women and old men were coming out to greet us. This meant that the shaman and his party of hunters hadn't returned yet. I still had time!

"What did you catch? What did you catch?" The children swarmed around us, eyes sparkling with curiosity.

Even though I was happy to see them, I was afraid of their discovering Yuit. "We caught some lake trout." I tried to shrug them off.

"Show us, Liak! We want to see the fish you caught!"

"Later, when we unpack."

I had bundled Yuit up so that nothing, not even her face, showed. Still, I was terrified she wouldn't be safe from the prying eyes of the children. She would only be safe once we could get her into Grandpa's *karmaq*. We had to head for it fast.

I saw Apitok smile at me and I smiled back. She was the only one I could trust with my secret. Later, after the excitement had died down and everyone had returned to their *karmaqs*, I would tell her. I was sure she would help me keep an eye on Yuit.

"What's in the bundle, Liak?" asked one of the boys, as he stared at it.

Before I could stop him, he poked it with his finger. "It moved!" he cried out, astonished.

Immediately, all the kids came pressing around the sled, touching and squeezing the bundle. "It's moving! It's moving! What is it?"

Grandpa came to my rescue. "It's only Liak's seal pup," he told them, his voice casual, so they'd lose interest and go away. "Later, she'll tell you all about it. Not now. We're tired. Please move out of the way so we can go home. Grandma's waiting for us."

Some of the kids moved away obediently, but others didn't. Soon, they were all back again, pressing around the sled and blocking our way.

"Liak, did you catch the pup all by yourself?" they asked, amazed.

"Grandpa helped me," I said, pushing my way through them and pulling the sled after me.

"Show us! Show us!" some of them pleaded.

"How did you catch it?" others asked.

By this time, some of the old men, too, had become curious. They perked up at the mention of a seal pup. Eating seal meat would be a welcome change from the boring diet of summer fish.

I felt an explanation was immediately necessary. "It's only a baby seal," I told them, as calmly as I could, "and I want to keep her as my pet. You'll all have lots of seal meat when Grandpa fetches the huge cow we cached. He harpooned the pup's mother."

My explanation worked! The old men nodded understandingly and moved away. But the children still milled around. I was afraid Yuit would suffocate and was anxious to remove the seal skin covering her. I had only made a tiny hole in it. "Please go away," I begged.

They wouldn't budge. The boys started prodding the pup with sticks and spears.

"Don't do that!" I cried out, horrified.

"We only want to help you kill it," they teased.

"Don't you dare hurt Liak's pup!" Grandpa's voice was heavy with anger.

They backed off.

"Aough! Aough!" Yuit's bark came through the seal skin, muffled but fierce.

Afraid, the boys put down their sticks and spears, but they still hung around.

"Don't worry, Liak," comforted Apitok, touching my arm. "We'll help you protect your pup."

"Can we take a peek at her, please?" one of the other girls begged.

"Later," I promised.

Grandpa and I reached our *karmaq* after what seemed like forever. We couldn't take the sled inside because the entrance was too small, so we hurriedly untied the skins covering Yuit and carried her in.

"Aough! Aough!" she barked, relieved to be free of those smothering seal skins.

One of the girls managed to squeeze in between Grandpa and me and caught a glimpse of Yuit's shimmering fur. "She's pure white like the falling snow!" she squealed with delight.

Immediately, all the other kids came running, pushing and shoving to take a look. "The pup's white! The pup's white!" They started dancing around and chanting excitedly. "Liak, can we play with your white seal pup?"

Before Grandpa and I could carry Yuit into our *karmaq*, some of the old men came hurrying over to see what all this new fuss was about.

"Yes," one of them murmured, as he bent down and touched Yuit's shiny fur, "she's truly white. Amazing for a ringed seal pup this age." Then his face changed, and he straightened up with fright. "Are those pink eyes I see?"

Another old man came to take a closer look. "It's an albino!" he cried out, aghast.

This immediately brought all the old men crowding around. "We must get rid of this pup before she brings bad luck to our camp!" they declared, their voices trembling.

And they grabbed Yuit from my arms and shoved her away, ignoring my desperate pleas.

The Debate

"Leave the pup alone!" Grandpa's voice was full of authority.

I felt proud of him. He still had control over the old men. They respected him because he was once the best hunter in the camp, better than they were.

"Thank you, Grandpa," I said, gratefully, as he helped me take Yuit away from the old men's clutches.

"Let Liak play with Yuit for a while," he told them. "When she's ready, she'll return the pup to Nuliajuk."

"It had better be soon," they cried out, angry at being thwarted, "or the shaman will surely banish your granddaughter when he returns!"

At the mention of the threat of banishment, Grandma gasped and pulled me to her, holding me protectively in the circle of her arms.

"Don't worry." Grandpa touched her shoulder comfortingly. "I'll talk to the *Angatkok* as soon

59

as he returns and explain everything to him. I'm sure he'll understand."

"Aough! Aough!" Yuit barked, wanting to be friendly as she moved towards the old men.

They looked uneasily at her pink eyes and backed away hurriedly. "You don't have too much time to indulge your granddaughter," they scolded Grandpa. "If the *Angatkok* and the hunters come upon a good herd of caribou, they'll have so much meat they'll be back in less than a week!"

"But if the caribou is scarce like it was last season, they won't be back until at least two weeks later," Grandpa said evenly.

"Why do you give in to your granddaughter so easily?" they scowled. "You're only spoiling her!"

When I heard this, I became upset. They were all picking on poor Grandpa, just because he was being kind to me. "He doesn't spoil me!" I defended him.

"You see!" they complained to one another. "She's insolent! She even argues with her elders!"

"And when the Sea Goddess finds out about the albino seal pup," one of them, who hadn't said anything up to this point, growled at Grandpa, "she is going to get so angry, she'll chase all the caribou away from our hunters. They'll be forced to come home empty-handed, hanging their heads in shame! And all because of this granddaughter of yours!" He wagged a finger at me.

All the old men glared at me, eyes flashing.

Grandpa realized that unless he soothed and humoured them, they would continue to harass me. I knew Grandpa well. He didn't want to fight with them because that would cut them off. He wanted them on his side when the shaman returned, so that they would back him up. He needed their moral support. "Prepare a feast," he told Grandma in the old men's hearing. "Serve the tea we brought back and our choicest pieces of seal meat with it." Then he turned to the old men. "You're all invited! Please share my food with me."

Immediately, they simmered down. They would never refuse a feast!

They moved aside as Grandpa brought Yuit, his camping gear and the seal meat inside our *karmaq*.

"Aough! Aough!" Yuit barked, as if thanking him, as she settled down quietly in a corner, watching us.

Grandpa was a clever negotiator, I thought proudly, as I followed Grandma into the *karmaq* to help her brew the tea and cook the meat. There was still enough flavour in the tea leaves to keep the old men happy. Everybody else in the camp had run out of tea. They were all waiting for the next trading trip up to Spence Bay to bring back some more. I could see the old men's eyes gleam as they looked forward to a steaming mug of tea. They sat just outside the entrance of the *karmaq*, waiting patiently while Grandma and I bustled about inside, cooking.

Grandma looked at the seal steaks I was cutting up and throwing into the large pot of broth on the primus stove. "There isn't enough meat there for everybody," she said. "I caught a ptarmigan yesterday while you were away. We should add the bird's meat to the seal steaks. That will make enough meat for everybody." She hurried to the cache just outside the *karmaq* and fetched the frozen bird. She cut it up and threw it into the boiling stew, looking satisfied.

When the tea was brewed and the meat cooked, she told Grandpa and he called the old men in. They sat down in a circle on the frozen floor. Laughing and talking politely now, they ate the food that Grandma and I served them in the tin bowls Grandpa had brought back from Spence Bay many years ago.

They lifted the bowls to their mouths and slurped the hot broth. They picked up the pieces of meat with the bone forks Grandpa had carved. They washed all this down with the steaming tea in tin mugs.

"It feels good to eat something other than fish!" they told Grandpa. Many asked for second helpings, chewing the meat and swallowing greedily.

"How did Liak find the albino seal pup?" they asked Grandpa, in between mouthfuls.

He told them about our hunting trip to the sea ice of Shepherd Bay, how we came upon and killed the seal cow and how we found her pup lying in the snow. "Don't worry," he assured them. "Liak will return the pup to the Sea Goddess as soon as it is ready to travel safely on its own."

They nodded, satisfied. Some even smiled at Yuit and me.

They stayed until all the food was gone; then they left, happy and smiling.

I was glad to see them go.

Saraak

Happy now, I divided my time over the next couple of days between learning to sew skins with Grandma and playing with Yuit. I made Yuit practice her tricks over and over until she became really good at them.

When the kids in the camp heard me laughing and singing with her, they flocked to my *karmaq*. They fussed over her. "You're so lucky to have found such a clever pet!" they told me. They laughed and clapped as she performed her tricks, encouraging her to go on. And she obliged because she loved nothing better than playing with us.

The kids would bring her gifts of fish. They were eager to teach her another trick. "Jump, Yuit! Jump!" they'd call as they dangled the fish above her. No matter how high they held the fish, she'd jump and catch it in her mouth.

Soon, Yuit and I became very popular in the camp. With Yuit and with all my new playmates, I no longer felt lonely. I only became sad whenever I thought of the *Angatkok*'s return. In this, I was not alone. The other children felt the same way. "We'll do all we can to help you," they promised.

I trusted them. All except one. She was a girl called Saraak. She wished she could have her own white seal pup. She was so jealous of me, she tried to hurt me by tormenting Yuit. She'd hold up a piece of fish. "Jump, Yuit! Jump!" she'd order. When Yuit jumped, she'd draw the fish away and laugh mockingly at the disappointed look in her pink eyes.

"Don't be cruel!" I'd scold her.

She'd merely stick her tongue out at me and make rude faces. She was growing more and more brazen. She'd poke Yuit with a stick and jeer as the pup moved away, frightened. She'd snatch away the snowballs that Yuit balanced on her nose. When Yuit sang her Aough Aoughs, along with the other children, she'd throw lumps of hard ice into her mouth, choking her.

"That's it!" I couldn't bear it any longer. "I don't want you coming to my *karmaq* anymore!" I was so angry, I chased her away.

"You'll be sorry!" she yelled as she ran out of the *karmaq*. "I'm going to tell the *Angatkok*! Just you wait!"

I ignored what she said. Why should I be afraid? She was just a mean, jealous girl. I had all the other kids on my side and, right now, we were all having too much fun playing with Yuit to bother about a troublemaker like her.

Not only did Yuit entertain the children, she also entertained their mothers. The mothers had heard so much about Yuit, they had to come and see for themselves. At first, they didn't believe, but when they saw her do her tricks, they became filled with wonder. Soon, they became so distracted they forgot all about their sewing. They would spend all day in Grandpa's *karmaq* playing with her. They'd never seen anything like her. They would laugh and clap just as excitedly as their children. When they returned to their *karmaqs*, they could talk of nothing else but her.

Because the women couldn't concentrate on their sewing, they began to make mistakes and their winter clothes began to look sloppy. They had to unpick and resew many of the skins, throwing away the damaged ones.

When the old men saw all this waste, they became furious. "Caribou skins are too precious to throw away!" they scolded the women. "We hardly have enough to wear! Don't you know that unless we have enough warm, skin clothing, we'll never be able to survive the long, cold winter months on the sea ice?"

A group of them rushed to see Grandpa, complaining bitterly. "You see, already your granddaughter's pet is bringing bad luck to our camp! Yuit is making the women throw away valuable skins. Without skins, we'll all freeze to death. She's also making the women late with their sewing. If the women can't sew our winter clothes in time, we'll never be able to leave for the sea ice to hunt seals. Without seal meat, we'll all starve. You must get rid of that pup at once!" They were so angry, they forbade the women and children from coming to see Yuit and me.

The atmosphere in the camp grew tense. The children became edgy. They were afraid for Yuit and me. Yet, there was little they could do. They had to listen to their elders. If they didn't, they'd be punished.

"I must do something about the situation," Grandpa said to me.

"How?" I felt depressed.

"I'll take the old men away with me to bring back the cached seal. They can't wait to eat more seal meat. On the way back, we'll check the trap lines for white fox. If we've trapped some, they'll have fox meat as well. That should keep them happy for a while."

"When will you be back?" I felt uneasy about

his going away.

"In two days. Don't worry about the *Angatkok*. I'll be back before him."

After Grandpa took the old men away, camp life returned to normal. The children began to flock back to see Yuit and, once again, their laughter could be heard all over the camp.

Two days later, I heard cries of welcome outside our *karmaq*. I heard the running steps of women and children pass by. "Grandpa's back!" I turned happily to Grandma. I put down my sewing and rushed out to see.

What I saw made me gasp. There, just rounding the bend of the river, I saw the *Angatkok*, and he was leading the band of hunters home.

The Angatkok

I shrank back into the shadows of my *karmaq*. Even from where I was hiding, I could feel the *Angatkok*'s tremendous power.

As I looked out, I saw his face was stern. For the first time since I had brought Yuit home, I understood what real fear meant. It made me feel small and helpless, like a snowflake being whipped around in a storm. I shivered. The *Angatkok* had the power to order me to be killed if I disobeyed him!

"My poor child!" Grandma put her arms around me.

"Ai! Ai!" I could hear the *Angatkok* holler at his dogs, forcing them to run faster.

Yuit nuzzled against my leg. "Aough! Aough!" she consoled me.

Feeling the warmth of Yuit's touch, all the energy that had drained out of me when I first saw the *Angatkok* flowed back into me. I felt as if I had just recovered from an illness.

I looked at the *Angatkok*'s sled and saw what it was that had brought him back so early. His sled was loaded with caribou meat and skins, and his dog team was struggling to pull it. All the other hunters' sleds were also loaded down with meat and skins.

"If only the hunting season had been bad, the *Angatkok* would never have returned before Grandpa," I said dejectedly.

"Cheer up," Grandma said kindly. "Grandpa will be back soon. I know it. He always keeps his word." She gave me another hug. "Look, I can see your father and brothers looking for you. Why don't you go and welcome them? It'll make you feel a lot better."

I was torn. I wanted to greet my father and brothers. Yet, I was afraid to show myself in case someone accidentally asked me about Yuit in front of them. On the other hand, if I kept away, my father and brothers would wonder where I was and would ask after me. Then what would happen if one of the kids let slip that I was looking after an albino seal pup in my *karmaq*? I couldn't take that chance.

"Aough! Aough!" Yuit agreed.

"I'll stay here and watch her for you," Grandma offered.

"All right," I said. "I'll go."

The hunters were smiling and handing out

delicacies to the children milling around them. My mouth watered as I saw the children munch on the green, undigested contents of caribou stomachs and chew on those big, juicy caribou eyes. I hadn't tasted such delicacies since last autumn! I'd better hurry before they were all gone.

"Where's Grandpa?" my father asked, when I ran over to him.

"He's gone with the old men to fetch the seal cow he cached."

"More meat!" he grinned. "Here," he said, handing me a couple of large caribou eyes.

"Thank you! I'll suck on them slowly and make them last as long as possible!"

He and my brothers laughed.

"We've brought some sinews for Grandma." He looked around for her in the crowd. "Where is she? She said she had run out of thread."

"She's resting in the *karmaq*. Can I take the sinews to her?"

"Sure." He handed me the small bundle of sinews.

Then he turned to his dog team. "Ai! Ai!" he called. The dogs took up the slack and began to pull the sled. I could see he was anxious to return to his *karmaq* and unload. Later, after he and my brothers had unpacked and fed the dogs, they'd visit Grandpa's *karmaq*, bringing gifts of meat and skins. There would also be some of Grandpa's favourite antler for him to carve.

As I raced back to my *karmaq*, I started to worry about Yuit once again. I didn't want my father to see her before Grandpa returned.

Grandma too felt the same way. "You should hide her," she told me anxiously.

"There's nowhere to hide her, Grandma! She has to remain here in the *karmaq* with me. If I hide her outside in the snow, the dogs will smell her out. They'd start howling and alert the hunters! And then what will happen?"

Grandma sighed. The lines on her face grew heavy and deep. She looked as if she were struggling with something inside her. "Liak," she said at last, "I was hoping that by now you would have tired of Yuit and let her go."

"No, I'll never tire of Yuit! She's my pet! I'll never let her go!"

"Not even if I gave you another pet like a puppy?"

"Never." I shook my head.

"I wish you wouldn't be so stubborn!" she said, losing her patience then. "I hate to think of what the *Angatkok* will do to you!"

Banished

Just then, I heard muffled footsteps in the snow outside. "That doesn't sound like Grandpa," I said. I immediately jumped up to hide Yuit.

Before I could push her under some skins, Apitok came rushing into the *karmaq*.

"Apitok! What's the matter? You look as if you've just seen an evil spirit!"

"Hurry! You must hide Yuit!" she cried, breathless. She had been running and was trying to catch her breath.

"Sit down, child," Grandma said, "and tell us what has happened."

Apitok was too upset to sit down. "It's Saraak!" she blurted out. "I never trusted her!"

I fought back the nervousness rising within me. "What did she do?"

"She told the *Angatkok*!"

I felt as if a rock had hit my head. "How did you find out?"

"As soon as the *Angatkok* returned, I followed Saraak everywhere. When the *Angatkok* went into his *karmaq*, she went in after him. I hid just outside the entrance, and I heard her tell him you were hiding an albino seal pup in your *karmaq*. I didn't wait to hear any more. I left immediately to warn you."

"You and Yuit must hide right away," Grandma told me, her voice urgent. "The *Angatkok* will be here any minute. When he comes, I'll tell him you're out playing with your friends. I'll stall him until Grandpa returns."

"No matter where we hide," I said, feeling my spirits sink, "the *Angatkok* will find us. Especially now that he knows the truth."

"Oh no! Here he comes!" Apitok gasped. "Liak, come with me! Hurry! Bring Yuit!"

"It's too late." I felt the hairs on the back of my neck stand on end. "I'll have to face him myself." Before I could thank her, she had gone.

She wasn't a moment too soon. As I looked out, I saw the *Angatkok* come striding towards my *karmaq*.

He looked so fierce, even Grandma shook. "Sea Goddess," she prayed, "please protect Liak."

"Aough! Aough!" Yuit pulled herself over to Grandma and comforted her.

Gratefully, Grandma reached down and touched her soft fur.

As I looked at Yuit, tears came to my eyes. Her beautiful, chubby face, with the blunt snout of a baby sea, was upturned, her pink eyes resting fondly on Grandma. She was so white and cuddly. I was overcome by my affection for her. I wanted to protect her always. Courage surged through me.

I turned and watched the *Angatkok* approach. He had strong muscles and was swifter than a caribou. His boots crunched the ice to powder as he ran. A moment later, I saw his sturdy legs close-up. They were standing right at the entrance to my *karmaq*. Then the light was blocked out as he crouched down and crawled in through the low entrance. Once inside, he stood up.

"Please sit down," Grandma said nervously. "I'll prepare you something to eat."

"No, thank you." He brushed her off gruffly. His eyes gleamed black and angry as he looked around the *karmaq*. They flared up like black flames the moment he saw Yuit. He glared at her pink eyes and her white fur. "So it's true!" His voice boomed like thunder rolling across the tundra. "Liak has been hiding an albino seal pup in her *karmaq*!"

I threw my arms protectively around Yuit.

"Where's Grandpa?" he turned to Grandma.

She told him where he'd gone with the old men. "He said he'd be back today."

He turned to me. "Didn't your Grandpa tell you it's bad luck to bring an albino seal pup into the camp?"

"Yes, he did."

"And you dared to disobey him?"

"Please," Grandma broke in, "Liak didn't mean any harm. She's innocent. She only wanted to protect the pup. She was afraid the dogs would kill the pup if she let her go."

I saw Grandma tremble; her face looked like the surface of the river when a strong wind blew across it. It made me feel guilty that I was causing her so much pain. It also made me look up directly into the *Angatkok*'s beady eyes. "Yuit is a very special pup," I heard myself say. "The Sea Goddess wants me to look after her and to be kind to her. That way, I'll be helping to make up for the past cruelty of the Inuit when they threw Nuliajuk out of their rafts and let her drown in the inlet."

"What an insolent girl!" the *Angatkok* glared at me furiously.

"Please." Grandma tried desperately to reason with him. "Grandpa will be back soon. He wants to talk to you."

"There's nothing to talk about!" He dismissed

her. "Liak must be punished!"

He turned to me, face hard as granite. "You have disobeyed my command, the command of an elder! You are guilty of bringing an albino seal pup into the camp, even though you were warned by Grandpa and the camp elders of the danger you would be facing. I cannot have mere children in my camp flouting my orders! If that were to happen, there would be no law and order around here. Because you have committed a serious wrong, I henceforth banish you from our tribe. You must leave early tomorrow morning. Let what has happened to you be an example to the other children. And," he jabbed a finger at Yuit, "you have until dark to get rid of this pup! I'll be back as soon as the twilight edges into dark. If the pup is still here, I'll order you to be put to death with an arrow! Yuit will be taken away to the ocean and returned to the Sea Goddess."

"But Liak's only a child!" Grandma sobbed. "Please don't be so harsh on her! Please give her another chance! I beg you! For Grandpa's sake, please! He loves his granddaughter so!"

Her pleas fell on deaf ears. The *Angatkok* turned away. "I'll return at dark!" he repeated to me.

Then, as abruptly as he had entered, he left.

Running Away

Istared after the retreating figure, my eyes unseeing. Even though I had known all along what would happen to me if I insisted on keeping Yuit as my pet, when it actually happened, I couldn't believe what I'd heard. I felt numb with shock.

"Get rid of Yuit," Grandma begged. "It'll show the *Angatkok* you're sorry and he might forgive you and allow you to stay. It's your only chance!"

"No, Grandma. I can't do that. Nuliajuk wants me to look after Yuit. One day, soon, she's going to tell me why."

"Think about what you're saying, child! Banishment is a terrible punishment! I'll get you another seal pup, a pure white one that isn't an albino. Then, perhaps, Grandpa can plead with the *Angatkok* to have mercy on you."

"No," I shook my head again. "I've made up my mind. I'm running away with Yuit."

"Where to, child?"

"To Spence Bay. The missionary who stayed here a long time ago will help me."

"You can't run away to Spence Bay alone! It's too far. You won't be safe. Why don't you wait till Grandpa returns? He'll help you get there."

"There's no time." I glanced outside. "It's almost dark. I must leave right away." I grabbed Yuit and hurried out.

"Wait! Take some food," said Grandma, trying to stop me.

"Food's too heavy to carry." I looked uneasily around me. I thought I heard the *Angatkok*'s footsteps returning. "Don't worry about me, Grandma. Grandpa taught me how to hunt. I knew it would come in handy one day! I'll find all the food I need along the way!" I raced away from the *karmaq*, turning back one last time to wave at her.

"I'll send Grandpa after you!" I heard her voice brush my ears like a comforting summer breeze. The tears came then. It was hard to leave Grandma behind.

Still, I had to put as much distance as I could between the *Angatkok* and myself. "Stay close, Yuit!" I whispered. "I don't want to lose you in the dark."

"Aough! Aough!" she barked, but she seemed to understand and struggled to keep up with me.

As I ran, I felt a depression like a black winter cloud press down heavily upon me. Already, I missed the camp; I missed Apitok and all my other friends. The ache grew worse the further away I ran. Banishment had cut me off completely from home and family. Now, I was truly alone. This realization filled me with fear. I'd never see Grandpa and Grandma again! Only now did I understand how much they meant to me and how much I had taken them for granted.

"Aough! Aough!" Yuit sympathized. She drew up alongside me and nuzzled my legs.

I reached down and touched her cold, comforting snout. "Yes, I know," I sobbed, "it's foolish of me to cry like this when I have you for company."

Try as I would, I couldn't shake off the feeling of insecurity. It was crushing me. What if the missionary didn't recognize me? What if he no longer lived in Spence Bay? Once, when I was there with Grandpa on one of his trading trips, he had pointed out the Catholic mission where Father Dubois worked, but I had been so busy chatting with my cousins, I hadn't paid too much attention. What if I couldn't find the mission now?

Several hours later, Yuit nudged me with her snout. "Aough! Aough!" She was telling me it was time to stop and rest.

I had been so engrossed in my thoughts, I hadn't realized how late it was, nor how far we had travelled. Only now, when I thought about it, did I realize how tired I was. Worse still, Yuit and I hadn't found a place to sleep for the night. We might get attacked by wolves!

"Aough! Aough!" Yuit poked at something with her snout.

I reached out with my hands, groping in the dark to find out what it was. I felt the shape of a snowdrift. It was as high as an igloo. "Yuit, if the snow is soft, we'll be able to dig." I examined the snow, feeling it with my fingers. "It's still soft! Let's dig, Yuit!"

Together, we started digging, Yuit with her snout and front flippers and I with my hands. We made a hole just big enough for the two of us. Then we crawled inside and snuggled up together.

Yuit's soft fur kept me warm. I felt drowsy. Soon, I drifted off to sleep with my arms around Yuit.

Who Could It Be?

Ididn't know how long I had been asleep. Suddenly, the silence was shattered by Yuit's barking. "Quiet, Yuit! I don't want anyone discovering our hideout." I peered out of our little cave. It was still dark outside. I couldn't see anything. I prayed it wasn't the *Angatkok* following us.

"Aough! Aough! Aough!" Yuit kept on barking even louder. She wriggled away from my grip.

"Come back, Yuit!" I cried out, scared.

She ignored me. She disappeared out of the hole, still barking as loudly as she could. Why was she acting so strangely? She had never disobeyed me before!

I heard a sled approaching. In the distance, I saw a storm lantern glowing in the dark. Who could it be?

"Yuit!" I heard a familiar voice.

I crawled out from the cave and ran towards the glowing lantern. "Grandpa! I'm here!" I cried out joyfully.

"I've been searching for you all night!" he said, relief in his voice as he hugged me. "If it hadn't been for Yuit barking and telling me where you were, I would never have found you! As soon as I returned home last night, Grandma told me what had happened. I left right away to find you."

In the light of the lantern, I could see his sled was still loaded high with his camping gear. He hadn't even stopped to unpack! He looked so tired. I felt sorry for him. "Grandpa, why don't you come and rest in our little cave? If you still have those tea leaves, I'll brew you some tea."

"I could certainly do with some breakfast!" he said. He poked his head in our cave. "So this is where you've been hiding!" He was impressed. "It's cozier than an igloo!" He made the cave a little bigger, to give himself enough room, and came in.

I served tea and some of the frozen seal meat and fish he had brought. Everyone, even Yuit, ate greedily. Because we were so hungry, food had never tasted better!

"I trapped a couple of white fox," Grandpa told me. "We'll save that for our journey to Spence Bay. Grandma told me you were headed there to see Father Dubois. I'll take you to him. He'll be able to find a safe home for Yuit.

And you and I can visit our cousins."

My earlier doubts disappeared. With Grandpa, I wouldn't feel so lonely and frightened.

When we had finished eating, we packed everything back on the sled. We tied Yuit securely on her bed of skins and sped away.

"We'll head west down the Murchison River," Grandpa told me, "and then north past Inglis Bay and Shepherd Bay to Spence Bay. Think of it as just another hunting trip and you won't feel so upset about being banished."

This cheered me up. But when I looked at Grandpa's leg and saw him still limping from our last trip, I started to fret again. "Are you sure your leg is all right?"

"Don't worry about it. It's just that I need some rest. I'll get lots of it when we arrive at Spence Bay."

I forced myself to stop worrying by thinking about other things. "Do you still have only six bullets left?" I pointed to his gun sticking out of the top of his hunting bag.

"Yes. I'll get some more from the trading store in Spence Bay."

It was fun travelling with Grandpa. He gave me lots of interesting tips along the way, and it felt just like old times. We crossed many long, narrow, frozen lakes and Grandpa showed me how to cut perfect ice holes with the snow knife. We fished for lake trout through these ice holes and caught enough to feed us all.

Two days later, we reached the sea ice of Inglis Bay. As we headed north, Grandpa explained why it was best to keep to the rough ice near the shore rather than walk on the flat ice further out near the water's edge. "Rough ice is old and well-packed," he said, "and it's safe to walk on. Flat ice is young. It's thin and dangerous. It cracks and piles up suddenly, crushing anyone who's unlucky enough to be caught in it."

"But polar bears also travel on rough ice," I reminded him, as I looked uneasily behind me. "What if one is following us?"

"If that happens, we can easily hide amongst the mounds and ridges in the rough ice."

One evening, after we had been travelling up the coast for several days, we stopped, as usual, to hack out blocks of ice and build our igloo for the night. After Grandpa had finished building our igloo, he went outside to unload his sled. While he was doing that, Yuit and I remained inside the igloo to pack down the snow for our sleeping platform. When we came out to see what was keeping Grandpa, we found him bent over his sled still fussing with his camping gear. He looked up. "My hunting bag," he said to me, pointing to where it lay on the ice. "Please put the snow knives back in it and take it into the igloo."

I ran to do as I was told. Snow was falling thick and fast, dulling any kind of noise. The sudden quiet made me curious. I turned to look at Grandpa and froze with fright. He was still bending over his sled, filling his arms with bundles of fox meat and seal meat to take into the igloo, but looming over him, I saw a large, white shape.

The Polar Bear Fight

It was the largest polar bear I had ever seen. Its coat was shaggy and off-white, looking dirty against the pure white falling flakes. It had reared up on its hind legs behind Grandpa, only a few yards away. It looked like a towering pillar, one mighty paw raised, ready to attack him.

I was terrified. My mind raced. What could I do to save Grandpa? If I called out, I would alert the bear and it would kill Grandpa. The bear hadn't seen me yet. Clutching Grandpa's hunting bag, I pulled out his rifle. I edged towards him. I was glad it was snowing. The snowflakes deadened any crunching sound my caribou boots might make on the ice.

Just then, Yuit started barking loudly, "Aough! Aough! Aough!"

Quiet, I wanted to cry out. Then I saw the strangest thing I'd ever seen. Yuit had moved behind the bear and was biting its rump, distracting it from Grandpa. Only trained hunting dogs did that to corner a bear! And Grandpa had said that Yuit didn't bite! The bear growled and turned to protect its rump. Only then did Grandpa finally turn around. It was the chance I had been looking for.

"Here's your gun," I shouted, as I raced up to Grandpa.

He grabbed it, cocked it and aimed it at the bear.

Yuit barked louder and started nipping even more fiercely at the bear. The bear was eying Grandpa. Yuit bit once more. The bear turned to strike her with its paw and exposed its neck. Grandpa fired.

"Don't let it hurt my baby seal!" I cried out, running towards Yuit.

"Keep away!" Grandpa ordered. He fired again.

I heard a small thud as the bullet bounced off the bear's thick hide. I heard the bear's enraged growl. It turned and charged at Grandpa.

I ran and pulled out the harpoon Grandpa had stuck on the outside wall of our igloo. Yuit kept on barking, trying to bark louder than the bear was growling in order to frighten it. She was trying to get the bear away from Grandpa. Somehow, the bear's swipes hadn't touched her. I knew Grandpa had only four more bullets left in his gun. I hoped he would kill the bear quickly. Getting a good, close heart shot was difficult. I prayed for his aim to be accurate.

I saw Grandpa race to the bear's left side. I saw Yuit nip at the bear's right rump. Again, the bear turned towards Yuit, trying to get rid of her. It roared ferociously.

Tensely, harpoon at the ready, I waited.

The sound of Grandpa's next shot was like a thunder crack. The bear turned and charged in the direction of the report. That was towards Grandpa! Onward the bear came, full of rage. It would soon drop. Wasn't that burst of energy its death run?

It kept on coming.

There were only three more bullets left.

Grandpa had to get out of his spot fast. From the stories the hunters told, I knew that, because bears were left-handed, their left paws were quicker than their right ones. Grandpa would never be able to escape a mauling from that left paw. For a split second, I saw Grandpa wait till the bear was nearly upon him. Then he quickly ran to the bear's right side, confusing it.

I saw the bear come to a screeching halt, claws digging deep grooves in the ice, showering me with ice chips. Awkwardly, it swung to the right, all the time tearing the tundra's silence with its frightening roars.

From the concentration in Grandpa's eyes, I

could tell he was more determined than ever to bring the bear down. He had to stop that mad charge to save himself. I watched nervously as he waited for the angry creature to raise its head, as it reared up on its hind legs to maul him. As soon as the bear did that, he would shoot it in the neck from close range. At this moment, more than anything else in the whole tundra, I wished Grandpa had a more powerful rifle.

What was the matter with the bear? Why wasn't it doing what Grandpa was willing it to do? It just kept on coming without raising its head.

Desperate to stall the enraged animal, Grandpa jumped around and fired into its hindquarters.

Two more bullets left!

Then the polar bear did do something unexpected. It turned around and bit at the bullet wounds in its hindquarters. As it did so, it exposed its neck again. Grandpa fired.

Only one bullet left!

"Die! Die!" I pleaded. "Please die!" I was truly afraid for Grandpa now.

The bear came at him. Frightened for him, I started to sob hysterically.

Yuit barked and moved towards me, trying to console me.

I ran towards Grandpa.

The bear was upon Grandpa. It raised itself on its hind legs. Practically under the bear, Grandpa fired his last shot.

The polar bear started to fall. I reached Grandpa just in time, and, dropping the harpoon, I grabbed his arm and pulled him away from under the falling bear. I didn't know where I got the strength from, but I managed to yank him away just as the bear came crashing down upon the ice.

Yuit was close behind me and I realized my strength had flowed from her.

Grandpa was panting. For a moment, he grimaced with pain. He bent down and massaged his leg. Then he straightened up and, limping, he moved away from the dead bear.

"Aough! Aough!" Yuit barked. It was a happy bark.

"Yuit!" Grandpa turned to her. "Who taught you to hunt like that?"

Her pink eyes shone, and she barked a couple of Aough Aoughs in reply.

I laughed. I was happy to see Grandpa stroking my pet.

"The way she nipped at the bear's rump to distract it! I couldn't believe it! She was actually biting very hard!" he chuckled.

I could tell that, at last, he had realized that Yuit was a special pup.

"And you helped too." He patted my cheeks. "You handed me that rifle just in time. If it hadn't been for both you and Yuit, the polar bear would have killed me for sure."

We worked on the bear, Grandpa deftly skinning it, while at the same time showing me how.

"I'll stretch and cure this skin, the first chance I get," he said.

"You're a hero, Grandpa! All the hunters are going to envy you when they see this bearskin."

"You think they'll be sorry for not inviting me along to hunt caribou with them, do you?"

"Definitely! Now they'll have proof you're still a good hunter!"

He beamed. "And just think what I can get for this coat in Spence Bay!" he said.

"You'll be able to buy a more powerful gun, to protect yourself from bears, musk oxen, or wolverines; you'll be able to kill them with just one shot.

"Exactly!"

When he straightened up after skinning the bear, I saw he was limping quite badly. "Are you in pain?"

"Just a little. It's the same leg one of the hunters accidentally shot when we were hunting caribou several years ago."

"Why don't you rest?"

"Later, when we've finished with the bear."

We quickly finished cutting all the meat we needed for the trip. We dug a hole just big enough for the carcass and cached it. Then we removed all traces of blood from the surrounding ice so no other bears would get at our meat. Grandpa explained that bears have an excellent sense of smell and can smell blood from a long way off. Finally, we went inside the igloo, taking the bearskin with us to dry overnight.

"I'll cook some bear meat for supper!" I was enthusiastic. "We haven't tasted bear meat for such a long time. It's going to be delicious! You rest until it's ready." I made Grandpa lie down on the comfortable bed of sleeping skins.

But by the time the food was cooked, his leg had swelled so much, he couldn't walk. He was so ill, he couldn't even eat.

I was really worried. "You'll have to lie on the sled tomorrow, Grandpa. Yuit and I will pull you to Spence Bay to get help."

"No," he muttered quietly, shaking his head. "I'm much too heavy to pull."

"What do you mean, Grandpa?"

"I mean that tomorrow, at dawn, you and Yuit must leave for Spence Bay without me."

The Journey
To Spence Bay

"I can't leave you here in the igloo all alone, Grandpa! You need someone to look after you!"

"I can look after myself," he said, irritation in his voice. "I'll hold out until you can get help for me. Go to Father Dubois at once. Tell him where I am."

"What about our cousins? Shouldn't I tell them too?"

"Yes, but go and see the missionary first. Tell him to come and get me. He'll recognize you as soon as you mention my name."

I could see Grandpa was having difficulty talking. His words were slurring, running into each other. His eyes were glazing over. He was struggling to keep them open until he could give me proper directions to the Catholic mission. The effort was exhausting. The moment he finished, he lay back and fell asleep.

I felt miserable all night, worrying about him. Early the next morning, Yuit nudged me awake with her snout. It was time to leave. I glanced at Grandpa. He was still asleep. He groaned once as if in pain. I touched his forehead. It was burning. He had a high fever! I didn't know how long it would take me to get help for him, so I decided to leave all the food within easy reach for him. All I took was my knife. A knife was always handy, he had taught me.

With as little noise as possible, Yuit and I left the igloo. Outside, I strapped her to the sled and we sped away.

As I thought about Grandpa lying there sick and helpless on the sleeping platform, I felt a pain in my heart. The pain rose and I broke into uncontrollable sobs. I didn't want anything to happen to him. I was very close to him. He was the only true friend I had. If he died, a part of me would die too.

Then I remembered something he had told me on one of our hunting trips together. "Liak," his gentle voice had said, "it's important always to smile and be happy in this short life on the tundra. Why be sad? No Inuit truly dies. Our bodies undergo a change we call death. Our souls live on forever as spirits in paradise, watching over our loved ones."

Immediately, I felt better. His words were

consoling. I brightened up and as I did so, my fears fell away like layers of powdered snow being blown away by the wind. My energy returned and I hurried away north, pushing myself with all my strength, eager to seek help for him from his old friend, Father Dubois.

Whenever I got tired along the way, I would stop and rest. "A good hunter always knows when to stop," Grandpa had said. "Rest increases his speed and accuracy."

"Yuit, you're heavy to pull!" I panted, as we continued on our way after one of our rest stops. "You must be getting fat!"

"Aough! Aough!" she protested. She slid off the sled and refused to be pulled. Instead, she went in front of it and picked up the seal thong with her snout.

"Oh!" I caught on. "You want to pull me, do you? What a wonderful idea!" I couldn't help smiling as I harnessed her to the sled the way Grandpa harnessed the dogs. She was acting like one! She had discovered another trick. All on her own, too! "Ai! Ai!" I called, as I hopped on the sled and let her pull me.

This way, taking turns to pull each other, our travelling became more of a game than a chore. Grandpa had said I must always be cheerful and I was being exactly that!

Along the way, I saw rabbits and muskrats

dart busily about. I saw them burrow in the snow as they got ready to go underground for the long, cold winter. I chased some of them, trying to catch them for food, but they were too quick for me.

I came across the last of the caribou making their way south to the tree-line where they would stay for the winter. "See you next year!" I called out to them. They stopped and stared. I opened my eyes wide and returned their stares, teasing them. Grandpa had told me what curious animals they were, always stopping to investigate things, which was why hunters were able to shoot them so easily. I noticed their huge antlers branching out on top of their heads. I had to swallow hard, fighting back the emotion, because I thought how much Grandpa would love to carve those antlers into toys to trade for knickknacks in Spence Bay.

As I raced across the snow, I heard some animals bellow in the distance. I stopped. "Look, Yuit," I pointed, "musk oxen!"

"Aough! Aough!" she barked at them.

"Ssssh, quiet, Yuit! They might charge if they think we're going to attack them!" I kept her well away from them. "I don't like the look of their big, powerful horns. Those musk oxen could gore us to death if they got angry."

I didn't want to take any chances, even though Grandpa had told me that musk oxen wouldn't attack unless they felt threatened. I didn't trust them. Already, the males were forming a protective ring with their young and females in the middle of the ring, as they faced Yuit and me. I saw their long, shaggy, black hair blowing in the wind and felt, more than saw, their black, angry eyes upon us. "Let's get away!" I said and we raced on.

After a while, I slowed down to suck on some pieces of ice. "I'm hungry, Yuit. Let's stop."

"Aough! Aough!" She, too, was hungry.

I looked around to see what I could catch with the gorge I always carried in my jacket pocket. I treasured it because I had carved it myself. It was a bone needle, pointed at the ends, with a hole in the middle through which I had threaded a long line of caribou sinew.

I examined the ice cover on one of the frozen lakes. I found a spot where the ice wasn't too thick and cut a hole with my knife. I then took out my gorge and jigged for trout in the icy water below. I caught several fish, and Yuit and I had a feast. Fresh fish always tasted better than frozen fish.

I saw many sea gulls flying around looking for food. "Stay quiet, Yuit," I whispered, as I pushed her behind a snowdrift. "I'm going to trap a gull and I don't want you scaring it away."

"Aough! Aough!" she barked, lying down obediently.

I watched a gull circle a pinnacle of ice. "I'll catch that one," I whispered.

I covered the gorge with fish bait. Then I climbed up the pinnacle and laid the gorge on it. Holding on to the line, I climbed back down and hid behind a mound of ice. Just as I had thought, the gull swooped down and greedily swallowed the fish bait. The gorge stuck in its throat. I pulled the line, reeling the gull in like a fish, and caught it. I killed it deftly by wringing its neck the way Grandpa had shown me and ate it raw. I liked the taste of its tangy meat, but Yuit preferred to stick to fish.

"Where there are gulls, there are bound to be eggs," I told her. "I'm going to find some. Gulls like to build their nests in high places away from danger."

I climbed the various pinnacles and mounds of ice, searching, and, sure enough, I found nests full of eggs. I filled my pockets with eggs, which I would eat when I got hungry along the way.

Yuit and I travelled like this for three days. Each day, as soon as it got too dark to see, we'd stop and burrow into a snowbank and curl up for the night. Safe in our hideout, we'd hear wolves howling in the distance, and the wind whistling across the tundra, piling up more snow. Early the next morning, feeling energetic after a good night's sleep, we'd be off again.

Late on the fourth evening, we reached the outskirts of Spence Bay. I could see the lights of the settlement twinkling through the falling snow. "Look, Yuit, we've arrived!" I said excitedly.

"Aough! Aough!" She too was glad.

Father Dubois

After the vastness of the tundra, it took me a while to get used to the narrow, ice-covered streets of the settlement. The streets were hemmed in on either side by rows of small, wooden shops and houses. The stores were dark because it was past closing time, but the lamps in the houses were lit.

As we passed the houses, I could hear people speaking Inuit. It felt good to be amongst people again. I had always enjoyed it when Grandpa brought me here on his trading trips. I liked the bustle and the noise as people bartered skins and carvings for tea, sugar, flour and beads.

I left the wooden houses behind and came upon some igloos made of gravel and ice. Immediately, I knew I was travelling in the right direction. I only hoped Father Dubois would be home. I didn't know what I'd do if he were away on one of his preaching missions in the tundra.

I found the church with the tall steeple that Grandpa had described. Behind the church, I saw the small, wooden house where Father Dubois lived. I knocked on the door, but there was no answer. I pounded the door with my fists. I heard footsteps. The door opened and a small, white man in black robes peered out. He was old and bald, but still vigorous, with a thin grey beard. Behind him, on a small wooden table, I saw a lamp burning.

"Yes, my child?" He spoke Inuit.

Even though I couldn't recognize him at first because he had grown so old, I remembered that voice.

"Father Dubois! It's me, Liak!"

He stared at me, trying to recall where he'd seen me.

"Grandpa saved you from a bear five winters ago. You stayed with us in our igloo and told me all about seals!"

"Liak!" His eyes sparked into recognition. "Ah, yes! Now I remember. How you've grown! No wonder I couldn't recognize you." He looked behind me. "Where's Grandpa?"

"He's ill. He needs your help fast."

"Oh dear. Come in and tell me what happened. Your Grandpa knows there's nothing I wouldn't do for him."

Just then Yuit barked, "Aough! Aough!"

"Did you bring a live seal with you?" He looked at the sled, surprised.

"She's my pet. She's called Yuit."

He helped me bring Yuit into the house and closed the door behind us.

"Aough! Aough!" Yuit nuzzled against his robes.

"She's a friendly one, isn't she?" He patted her snout. He looked at me closely in the light of the lamp. "My poor child, you look hungry and tired! I'll fix you something to eat."

While he was busy making tea, frying bannock bread and spreading thick layers of jam on it, I told him my story. Twice, I blinked back tears.

"I'm sorry about what happened to you," he said with sympathy. "I'll do all I can to help."

I described the exact location where Grandpa lay. By the time I had finished talking, the food was ready.

"Sit down and eat," he said.

He gave Yuit some raw fish.

"Aough! Aough!" she barked, as if thanking him, and gobbled it down.

"What a polite seal!" Father Dubois chuckled.

"Yes, she is," I agreed. "She's so easy to look after and such a good pup. I need to find a good home for her where she can be happy and where I can watch over her. Can you help me?"

"I'll certainly do my best," he promised.

After we'd eaten, he showed us where we could sleep. It was a small room behind the kitchen, which he used as both a storage room and a guest room. He moved the books, the cartons of tea, sugar and flour aside and threw a mattress of skins on the floor. "As soon as you and Yuit have settled down for the night, I'll leave with my dog team to fetch Grandpa."

"But I'm coming with you!" I insisted. "I'll show you where he is."

"That won't be necessary, my child. I know the area very well. I've preached in it for years. You stay here and get some sleep."

"How long will it take you to fetch Grandpa?" I thought of poor Grandpa all alone and starving because he was too ill to eat.

"If I travel all night, I should be back with him by tomorrow evening. My six dogs are excellent runners. And now, you and Yuit must go to sleep. Good night." He smiled and left the room. He was in a hurry to leave.

I heard him turn off the lamp in the kitchen, and then all was dark. A little while later, I heard his dog team speed down the street. I listened until the sounds of his sled, scraping the ice, had faded away. Then I lay down on the mattress, with Yuit on the floor beside me.

It was hard to go to sleep. Everything around

me was so strange and different. Father Dubois was kind, but I felt out-of-place here in his house. I hated being banished. The tears started to come again. There was no one to see me, so I let them flow freely; they helped get some of my pain out. I thought of Grandma and Grandpa. I missed them both terribly. I thought of Grandpa lying sick in the igloo far away. For a long time, I stared, red-eyed, into the darkness, wondering if Father Dubois would reach him in time.

Would I Be Accepted?

Already, I could feel my life was changing. It had started the moment I was banished. I had left behind my traditional way of life, where my people migrated from camp to camp with the seasons, hunting and fishing for our food. Here, in Spence Bay, I was faced with the modern way of life, where the Inuit worked in stores to earn money to buy food. They lived in little, wooden houses instead of igloos. I wasn't sure I was going to like this way of life. It was a new experience and it scared me.

I felt uncomfortable sleeping in a house made of wood. I wasn't used to the smell of wood and I didn't like it. A wooden house made me feel cooped up. It felt stuffy. I preferred to sleep in an igloo, where I could touch the solid snow and ice all around me with my fingers. And I could breathe in the biting, fresh, cold wind, as it whistled through the entrance and out through the small opening in the igloo's ceiling.

Yet, if I was going to live in Spence Bay, I had better get used to sleeping in a wooden house. My cousins lived in one at the other end of the settlement. As I slowly drifted off to sleep, I wondered whether they would invite me to live with them when I visited them tomorrow. Would they take Yuit in, too?

The next morning, I was wakened by an Inuit woman banging loudly on the door. "Father Dubois told me to cook your breakfast," she said, when I opened the door.

Breakfast for me consisted of fried fish, fried bannock bread and a mug of tea. There was frozen fish for Yuit.

The woman waited until we had finished eating. Then she cleaned up and left.

I was glad to see her go. I wondered if the people in the settlement were like her, cold and unfriendly. What if they didn't accept me? I wanted to be liked and accepted so badly by the people I was going to live with.

"Yuit, I'm going to talk to my cousins. Stay here. I'll be back soon. I don't want strange people staring at you in the streets."

"Aough! Aough!" she agreed, even though I could see she didn't like being left alone in an unfamiliar house.

Head braced against the icy wind, I hurried down the streets to the other end of the settlement where my cousins lived. Their father, Audladjut, was my mother's cousin. He had married a woman from Spence Bay called Tinatluq. They had six children. Two of the girls, Tiliq and Nagtok, were about my age. Three of the boys were younger and the oldest sister worked in a store selling sugar and flour.

"Where's Grandpa?" Audladjut and Tinatluq asked when I arrived. They were surprised to see me alone. When I told them everything that happened, they took pity on me.

"Try not to worry about anything," they said, calming my fears. "Grandpa is in good hands. Everybody here loves and trusts Father Dubois. And as for you not having a home or family to go back to, you can certainly stay with us. We'll look after you as if you were one of our own children. But we can't keep Yuit. We're poor and we don't have food to spare for a pet. Neither do we have the room for two extra. "

Although I was glad my cousins had accepted me, I was sad they couldn't help Yuit.

"Liak, can we come and see your pet?" Tiliq and Nagtok asked me, curious, after I'd finished talking with their parents and was ready to leave.

"Of course!" I said. I couldn't wait to show Yuit off.

The three of us raced back to the missionary's

house.

"What a beautiful pup!" they cried, as soon as I opened the front door. "Such shiny fur! And those eyes!" They couldn't get over Yuit's glowing pink eyes. They sat on the floor and romped with her.

Yuit enjoyed the fuss they were making, and showed her pleasure by thumping her tail on the wooden floor. "Thump! Thump! Thump!"

"And now, here's a surprise!" I announced. "Do your tricks for my cousins, Yuit!"

Tiliq and Nagtok squealed with delight as Yuit rolled over and over on the floor, balanced a snowball on her nose, clapped her flippers and sang her Aough Aoughs. "How we wish she could stay with us!" they cried.

When it was time for them to go, they hugged Yuit. "We'll be back soon," they promised.

Late that evening, when I was just starting to despair, I heard a sled scraping ice in the distance and dogs howling. "Father Dubois is back, Yuit!"

Together, we ran out of the house and down the street to greet him. When I looked at the sled, it was empty. My heart missed a beat. "Where's Grandpa?" My voice sounded shrill and despairing.

"I took him to the nursing station here in Spence Bay. He has bronchitis and a high fever. He also has a torn muscle in his left leg. But don't worry. The doctor said he'll be better in a few weeks."

"Thank you for helping him!" I felt relief sweeping through me, glad that Grandpa was going to live.

As we walked back to the house, I told Father Dubois about my visit with my cousins.

"And will you be happy living with them?"

"Yes."

"I'm glad. You'll be amongst your own relatives and you won't feel so lonely. You know you can always come to me whenever you need help. All we have to worry about now is Yuit."

School

When Father Dubois returned home from saying Mass in church the next morning, he was accompanied by the Constable of the Royal Canadian Mounted Police. "He's in touch with everyone who comes in and out of Spence Bay," he told me. "Maybe he'll find a nice place for Yuit to stay."

"So this is Liak and her pup!" The Constable looked first at me and then at Yuit.

He didn't smile. He had a gruff manner. He reminded me of the *Angatkok*, and I shrank from him. He was a big man with red hair and a bushy red beard.

"Hmmmmmmmm," he shook his head at Yuit, frowning. "I don't know of too many places that will take in a seal pup."

"Aough! Aough!" Yuit barked at him. Then, before his astonished eyes, she went into her routine of tricks.

"Amazing!" he exclaimed, as his eyes bulged

until I thought they were going to pop out. "Such intelligence! Let me see...I think I have an idea..."

"And what's that?" Father Dubois asked.

I could see Father was protective of Yuit.

"Perhaps I can find an aquarium to take her in," the Constable replied. "It might be just the right home for her. The trouble is," he tugged on his beard, pulling some of the hairs out, "the closest aquariums I can think of are in Ontario and Manitoba. I'll write to them. I'm sure Yuit will be happy in an aquarium there."

"Aough! Aough!" Yuit shook her head.

The Constable stared at her, puzzled.

"She's telling you she won't go anywhere without me," I explained. "She's not only my pet. She's also my friend. She doesn't want to be separated from me."

"What a spunky pair! Now that creates a problem!"

"Surely, there must be another solution," Father Dubois insisted. "Liak and her pet cannot be separated."

"Let me think." The Constable scratched his beard. "Ah, yes. There's a marine biologist from Lord Mayor Bay who has just arrived to do some research on polar mammals. Maybe he'll have the answer. He's away right now. As soon as he returns, I'll go and talk to him."

So saying, he turned and left.

"The Constable may be abrupt," Father Dubois told me, when he'd gone, "but believe me, you can rely on him."

I wasn't so sure, but I thought it best not to say anything. I didn't want Father Dubois to think I was ungrateful.

"Is there something else on your mind, my child?" Father asked me.

"Yes. I want to go to school. It's something I've always wanted to do, but I could never talk to Grandpa about it. He doesn't think school is necessary for girls. My cousins, Tiliq and Nagtok, go to the government school here. They told me about all the fun they have and the number of friends they've made. Can I join them too?"

"Of course!" Father Dubois was enthusiastic. "I know the head teacher very well. I'll go and see him and make arrangements for you to be enrolled at his school."

I was overjoyed.

I couldn't wait to tell Grandpa when I went to visit him at the nursing station. He was already looking better after only a day there.

"Well, if you're going to live in Spence Bay with your cousins," he said, looking resigned, "you might as well do as they do. It's the modern way of life and it's important that you become a part of it." Then a faint smile flickered in his eyes. "I think you're ready for it."

"I think so too, Grandpa!" I agreed. Then I suddenly thought of something. "When you're better, are you going to stay here in Spence Bay with me?"

"I'll only stay until you're settled in your new life and Yuit has found a good home. Then I'll return to our tribe. I'm too old to change my ways."

I felt a pang of regret, but forced myself to understand. I knew Grandpa would always keep in close touch with me. He would always visit me on his trading trips here. The bond between us was far too strong to break just because he was returning to the old way of life and I was going on to the new.

Whenever I wasn't visiting Grandpa at the nursing station, I'd take Yuit and we'd go and see Tiliq and Nagtok at their house at the end of the settlement.

People would stop and stare every time I walked down the street with Yuit. No one in Spence Bay had ever seen a pet like her before. When they heard I'd been banished because of her, they showed concern and wanted to help. They were modern Inuit who no longer clung to their old beliefs. They didn't think an albino seal pup would bring bad luck. They accepted Yuit, and this pleased me greatly. Feelings of warmth for the people of Spence Bay began to surge through me.

"Show the people your tricks!" I'd encourage Yuit.

The people would crowd around, mouths falling open as they watched her show off what she had learned. "Amazing!" they'd chorus.

News of the amazing seal pup and her clever tricks began to spread across the whole settlement. Soon, people came from everywhere to look at her and cheer her on as she romped and showed off her skills. They were so impressed, they invited me into their homes and offered me food. This meant they had accepted me as one of their own.

"Sea Goddess," I whispered, "I think I'm going to be happy here in Spence Bay." I sniffed the wood from the houses all around me. "Even the wood is beginning to smell good!" I told her, my lips parting in a wide smile. Already, the strangeness of the settlement was melting away like snow in the summer sun.

The Ways Of Nuliajuk

One day, just shortly before I was to begin school, a stranger knocked on the door of the missionary's house.

"Aough! Aough!" Yuit greeted him as soon as I opened the door.

"So you're the white seal pup I've heard so much about!" he said, patting Yuit. "Everyone in Spence Bay is talking about you!"

"Aough! Aough!" she barked, as she thumped her tail happily on the floor.

The stranger laughed. "I'm Bill Anderson," he said to me. "I'm the marine biologist the Constable told you about. I talked with Father Dubois at the church this morning and he told me to come here and see you."

He was young and friendly and I liked him instantly. I could see how well he understood seals.

"I'm sorry about the delay," he apologized. "I only returned from Lord Mayor Bay yesterday, and the Constable came over right away to see me. He told me all about you and Yuit."

"Do you have a home for her?" I couldn't keep the anxiety out of my voice.

Before the marine biologist could answer, Yuit barked, "Aough! Aough!" grabbing his attention. As soon as he looked at her, she began to do her tricks, ending up with her Aough Aough song.

"Amazing!" he clapped. "She's the most intelligent seal pup I've ever seen! No wonder people are talking about her!"

"She's special," I said, my heart swelling with pride.

"I can see she is! I went to Lord Mayor Bay specially to look for a seal to act as a leader for my other seals, but I couldn't find the right one. This one is fantastic! Seals learn by imitating and with Yuit to help them, they'll learn fast. Of course, she can stay with me here at my research centre. She'll be a good example to the other seals."

"Thank you!" I felt ecstatic. I couldn't have asked for anything better. At last, I had found a good home for Yuit. She would be happy there with all the other seals for company. Also, she would be close to where I would be staying at my cousins' house. Tiliq, Nagtok and I could visit her everyday after school.

"I'm doing research on the intelligence of seals," the marine biologist continued, "and I can tell Yuit is going to give me a great deal of insight into that."

"Aough! Aough!" Yuit thumped her tail, agreeing.

"She's not shy, is she!" he grinned. "She loves attention." He stroked her thick, silky fur. Then he told me something that convinced me the Sea Goddess was looking after me. "You need have no fears," he assured me. "Yuit and her seal friends will have all the freedom they need to roam the sea ice behind my house. I love seals; they will not be subjected to any experiments. They can come and go as they please in their natural habitat. You can help me look after them, feed them and monitor their intelligence."

"I've always wanted to do that!" I confided.

"You've got the job, Liak! After seeing the way you've cared for Yuit, I'm sure you'll be able to mind the other seals just as well."

I was sure there was no girl in the whole tundra happier than I.

"Father Dubois told me you'll be staying with your cousins and going to the government school here," he continued. "When school is over each day, you can come over and help me care for and feed the seals, and you'll get paid for your work," he smiled. "It won't be much, but it'll give you an allowance."

I was thrilled. I didn't care how little it was. It meant I would be earning a living just like the rest of the Inuit here. I would be one with them, slipping into their way of life, and I was finding this change exciting. Grandpa was right. I was ready for this modern way of living. "I'll send the money home to Grandpa," I said. "Now that he has proved himself a hunter, he'll be needing his own dog team."

"Yes, he will. Father Dubois told me about that bear fight. Your Grandpa is a brave man."

"He is."

"And now, Liak, I have to go. I have work to do. My house and research centre is only a small, wooden building near the water's edge, but it means a lot to me. It's going to help me prove how very intelligent seals are. Tomorrow morning, I'll come and fetch Yuit. She'll love it there with the other seals. And remember," he smiled as he turned to go, "you can start work after school tomorrow!"

"I'll remember!" I called after him. I couldn't wait till tomorrow! I threw my arms around Yuit. "Everything is falling into place!" I danced around the room excitedly with her.

"Aough! Aough!" she barked. She too could hardly contain her excitement at the idea of her new life here in Spence Bay.

As I gazed at those glowing, pink eyes, set in a face of shimmering, white fur, I began to understand the ways of the Sea Goddess. Because I had been kind to her albino pup, the Sea Goddess was being good to me by helping me change my life for the better. If it hadn't been for Yuit and my banishment from my tribe, I would never have been able to go to school here. Now I would learn to read and write like the modern Inuit did. I would live like them in a house; I would have Tiliq and Nagtok for company; I would earn money for doing work; and I would meet lots of boys and girls my own age in school and visit with them in their houses. It would be fun! And because Yuit had saved Grandpa's life, I was sure the *Angatkok* would one day accept her. When that happened, I knew I myself would be forgiven and that meant I would be able to return to my people on the Murchison River, if only for visits.

"Thank you, Sea Goddess!" I whispered joyfully in my heart.

All my dreams had come true.